Praise for Barbara Delinsky

"...ara Delinsky knows the human heart and its im-
...e capacity to love and to believe."

Washington (PA) *Observer-Reporter*

"Delinsky is an expert at portraying strong women
characters." *Booklist*

"Delinsky is one of those writers who knows how to
introduce characters to her readers in such a way that
they become more like old friends than works of fiction." *Flint Journal*

"Delinsky is an engaging writer who knows how to in-
terweave several stories about complex relationships,
and keep her books interesting to the end. Her special
talent for description gives the reader almost visual
references to the surroundings she creates."

Newark Star Ledger

"Delinsky's prose is spare, controlled and poignant as
she evokes the simplicity and joys of small-town life . . .
She capably balances her narrative on the tightrope between spirituality and earthly love." *Publishers Weekly*

"Delinsky steers clear of treacle . . . with simple prose
and a deliberate avoidance of happily-ever-after
clichés." *People*

"Barbara Delinsky should touch even the most jaded
of readers." *Chattanooga Times*

"Delinsky creates . . . a remarkably beautiful story."

Baton Rouge Advocate

Books by Barbara Delinsky

Shades of Grace
Together Alone
For My Daughters
Suddenly
More Than Friends
A Woman Betrayed
Finger Prints
Within Reach
The Passions of Chelsea Kane
The Carpenter's Lady
Gemstone
Variation on a Theme
Passion and Illusion
An Irresistible Impulse
Fast Courting
Search for a New Dawn
Sensuous Burgundy
A Time to Love
Moment to Moment
Rekindled
Sweet Ember
A Woman's Place

BARBARA DELINSKY

Passion and Illusion

HarperTorch
An Imprint of HarperCollinsPublishers

This is a work of fiction. Names, characters, places, and incidents are products of the author's imagination or are used fictitiously and are not to be construed as real. Any resemblance to actual events, locales, organizations, or persons, living or dead, is entirely coincidental.

A previous edition of this book was published in 1983 by Dell Publishing Co., Inc., under the pseudonym Bonnie Drake.

❦

HARPERTORCH
An Imprint of HarperCollins*Publishers*
10 East 53rd Street
New York, New York 10022-5299

Copyright © 1983 by Barbara Delinsky
Excerpt from *A Woman Betrayed* copyright © 1991 by Barbara Delinsky
ISBN: 0-06-104232-3

First HarperTorch paperback printing: October 2002
First HarperPaperbacks printing: May 1994

HarperCollins ®, HarperTorch™, and ❦™ are trademarks of Harper-Collins Publishers Inc.

Printed in the United States of America

Visit HarperTorch on the World Wide Web at www.harpercollins.com

10   9   8

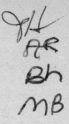

Passion and
Illusion

One

Monica Grant reached for a final book to add to the stack in her arms. She picked it up, skimmed the back-cover copy, then replaced it on the shelf. It was set in the Caribbean. She'd already chosen one story set there, plus several others that were set abroad. No, she mused, pensively studying the display before her, she was in the mood for something American, something contemporary, something dramatic. She pondered two other books before settling on a third and tucking it into the crook of her arm with the rest. Then she stole a glance to either side of her.

To her relief the aisle was still empty. The

bookstore itself was nearly deserted. There was a browser one row to the left in Games and Hobbies, another two rows to the right in Psychology, and several others scattered along the far Non-Fiction rack. She had Romance all to herself.

With a smile of satisfaction she snapped up a magazine to camouflage the selections nearest her heart, then at a more leisurely pace she ambled toward the best-sellers. A first and a second, each by authors she hoped to interview during their forthcoming publicity stops in Boston, topped the pile. Then, with another cautious glance around, she headed for the cash register.

Luck was on her side. There was only she and the clerk, a studious-looking young man who tactfully rang up her sales without commenting on either her choices or the sheepish look she was trying so hard to suppress. She half-wished he'd ask, then she might tell him the tale of her friend in the hospital who was hopelessly addicted to love stories. But he didn't ask, and she left well enough alone.

It was only when the books were all safely tucked into a bag and hidden from public view that she dared look the clerk in the eye. "Thank you." She smiled more comfortably.

He nodded. "Come again."

"I will," she said and knew that she would. Next week, next month, the month after . . . whenever her supply ran out, she'd be back.

Clutching her treasures to her breast, Monica stepped out into the bright midmorning sunshine, took a deep breath of pleasure, and turned to head for home. But just as quickly the breath was knocked from her lungs when a body barreled into her, throwing her against the concrete wall of the building. Stunned, she slid to the sidewalk, oblivious to the shouts around her until one deep voice came through, close by her ear.

"Are you all right, miss?"

She gasped in the struggle to catch her breath but didn't move from where she sat slumped against the wall, her legs curled beneath her, her arms gripping herself and her belongings protectively. Her head was bowed, sending curled ribbons of light brown hair cascading over her face like a screen, behind which she slowly regained her composure.

"Miss?" The deep voice came again, and a gentle hand drew back her hair. "Are you hurt?"

Eyes still closed, Monica shook her head.

"I don't think so," she whispered, but already she felt a stinging in her forehead, another in her shoulder.

"Can you stand up?"

Again she shook her head. "Give me a minute."

Her rescuer held her arm lightly as he reached into his shirt pocket. "Here. Press this to your head." Without a pause he did it himself. "You've scraped your temple. It doesn't look serious. Anything else hurt?"

Lifting a shaky hand, she relieved his hand and pressed the handkerchief to her temple. "My shoulder." Only then did she open her eyes to examine the damage herself. It might have helped if it had been winter and she had been bundled up to the hilt. But this was the middle of June, it was hot, and she wore a bare sundress that had offered no protection when she'd hit the wall. Her shoulder was badly scraped, and she could begin to imagine what her forehead looked like.

"Can you move your arm?"

She gave it a try and grimaced but succeeded. "It's okay. Just messy, I guess." Then she caught sight of the crowd gathered around in a semicircle and winced with distaste.

"Okay, folks." Her attendant understood

instantly that she needed privacy and gestured toward the crowd. "Move on now. She's all right."

When she heard the note of authority in his voice, Monica looked up for the first time at the man who'd come to her aid. He had crouched down beside her, one knee braced on the sidewalk. He wore navy-blue pants, a matching navy shirt with a badge on the breast pocket and the departmental insignia on its sleeve, and the standard patrolman's hat. Had it not been for the surprisingly warm depth of his brown-eyed gaze she might have stiffened on pure reflex. Instead she could only stare for a perplexed moment before gathering her strength to stand up.

He was right beside her, lending his firm support with a hand at her elbow, an arm at her waist. When it appeared that her legs would hold her, he released her. "Better?" His voice was as deep and as warm as his gaze.

"A little shaky . . . but, yes." She dabbed her forehead with the clean handkerchief he'd given her, folded it over, then replaced it on the swelling bruise. "I suppose I'll have a whopper of a headache later." She laughed weakly, feeling strangely self-conscious. "What hit me, anyway?" Chancing a glance past him, she saw that the crowd had dispersed, leaving no sign of a guilty party.

"A pickpocket" came the quiet reply.

Monica's eyes widened in disbelief as she raised them to meet the more penetrating gaze of the policeman. "*The* pickpocket?"

His lips twitched. "Unless my buddy catches him, we'll never know, will we?"

She followed the line of his sight up the street, then glanced down at her purse and the bag containing her books. Both appeared to be undisturbed. Involuntarily she hugged them closer. "I thought pickpockets were supposed to be subtle. Whatever hit me couldn't have known the meaning of the word."

To her chagrin the policeman chuckled. "You wouldn't pose much of a challenge to a pickpocket." His eyes skimmed her slender form, bringing a wash of color to her cheeks. "It doesn't look to me like you've got a pocket on you. Besides," he went on smoothly before she could react to his appraisal, "he wasn't looking for a victim. He was running from *us*."

Eyes flashing, Monica scowled. "That figures. Why is it that innocent people so often get hurt when you fellas get the urge for a chase?" She twisted her head around and peered at her shoulder in disgust.

Her hero was undaunted. "It's unfortunate

when it happens, but there's not much we can do when someone walks blindly into the fray the way you did." He paused long enough to convey a hint of doubt, which he then proceeded to express backhandedly. "I'm assuming it was pure coincidence."

"Coincidence?" she cried, glaring sharply up at his shaded face. "It was my *misfortune* is what it was. And if you're implying that I purposely wandered into something looking to get hurt—" But she suddenly understood his full implication and gaped at him openly. "Now, wait a minute—" Wincing, she recalled another time, another place, and couldn't suppress a shudder.

"Are you all right?" he asked again, more gently, concerned by her sudden pallor. He reached for her arm to steady her, but before she could respond his partner approached, visibly winded. "No luck?"

The newcomer removed his hat and mopped his brow with his arm. "Sorry, Mike. I lost 'im. He must know every street and alley around here. She have anything?" He cocked his head toward Monica, who wanted nothing more than to return to her nice cool apartment. She didn't like the heat. She didn't like the stares of the passersby. And she most definitely didn't like the police.

"I'm working on it now," the officer called Mike informed his partner as he turned back to Monica. Reaching into a back pocket, he withdrew a small notebook and flipped it open. "I'd like to ask you several questions, miss."

Monica sighed, trying to recall what a lovely morning it had been such a short time before. "Is this absolutely necessary? I'd really like to get going." A soft chair, a cool drink, and the first of those mind-pleasing novels sounded about right.

"It's necessary." He took a pen from his pocket. "Your name?"

Once more the past crowded in. "Why do you need my name?"

"Routine. You may be able to help us nab whoever-he-was." He cocked his head in the direction in which the suspect had vanished.

"But I didn't see him," Monica argued. "If I'd seen him, I might have avoided him. I wish I could help but—"

"May I see your purse?" he asked politely. Politely . . . but firmly.

She felt her hackles rise. "You may not! You can't just stop people on the streets and—"

"If I suspect an obstruction of justice, I can."

"Obstruction of justice? That's ridiculous! I

was in that bookstore very innocently buying books . . ." She remembered her books and tightened her arm around them.

The policeman had begun to take notes. "Now we're getting somewhere." His partner ducked away to retrieve the cruiser and call in to headquarters. "What happened then?"

Frustrated, she leaned back against the wall. "I paid for my books, left the store, and began to walk. Then . . . wham! You know the rest."

"Where were you headed?" He studied her closely. But she kept her mouth shut, annoyed at this invasion of her privacy. Bickering with him had gotten her nowhere. Silence might be more effective. Sensing her ploy, he lowered the notebook. "Do you work around here?"

She stared at him as defiantly as she could, trying to dislike him, succeeding only in acknowledging that he was the best-looking policeman she'd ever seen. Tall, tanned, and strong-featured, he had an air of refinement with which he could as easily have been a very proper Bostonian as a member of its police department. He was also persistent and very clever.

"Do you have something to hide?" he asked more slowly, narrowing his gaze in suspicion.

He'd asked the one question she couldn't let pass, for fear of incriminating herself. "Of course not!"

"Then tell me your name."

She hesitated briefly, wondering again how he could be a policeman. Those eyes . . . brown, almost golden in warmth . . . more persuasive than any legal threat. "Monica. Monica Grant."

"Monica Grant." He tested the sound, and she feared for an instant that he'd recognized it. But she used her middle name professionally. There had to be another reason for his pause. Then, as though recalling his duty, he jerked up the notebook and jotted it down. "Address?"

From here on he'd be able to learn it anyway. "One forty-five West Cedar."

"Ah. Beacon Hill."

"That's right." She waited for the typical gibe, but it never came. Rather, he lowered the notebook again.

"Nice area. Have you lived there long?"

She knew he had no business asking her this question but somehow found herself responding. "Four years now."

He smiled, and she felt rewarded. "You're not from Boston originally, are you? You speak differently." He seemed genuinely interested, less of a cop, more of a man. She couldn't help but return his smile.

"No more so than you." She thought she heard a twang in his speech, and it was a far cry from the usual Boston accent. "I'd guess . . . the Midwest?"

He arched a brow. "Not bad." But he would say no more. And at that moment his partner drove up, drawing the tall officer's attention first to the cruiser, then back to Monica. "I've got to go through your bags. There's a chance our pal may have dropped something on you."

"That's imposs—"

He held up a hand to stifle her outburst. "Without your knowledge, of course."

"I'm telling you that my things weren't touched."

"It's my job, Ms. Grant. Look at it reasonably. This whole area has been bothered by a mysterious hunt-and-peck thief for several months. If he managed to plant something on you, we may be able to get fingerprints. It's a start."

Though she knew this made sense, Monica still disliked the idea of being searched. "So . . . I'm the innocent victim again?"

He ignored the barb and took a step closer, speaking softly, almost intimately. "I realize that it may be embarrassing for you out here on the sidewalk. We can either sit in the car, go to your place or . . . head down to the station."

"The station?" she exclaimed, then quickly lowered her voice. "I'm not going to the police station. This is ridiculous!"

"Maybe so"—he held her gaze—"but I've got to check."

Feeling weary and suddenly aware of the throbbing at her temple, Monica lowered her head and closed her eyes. The pose of fatigue seemed to be the deciding factor.

"Come on. I'll give you a lift home. You could use some ice on that bruise." Without another word he took her arm and led her to the car, gently depositing her in the back seat before joining his partner in front.

It took less than five minutes to reach her apartment. Monica sat back helplessly, feeling herself the victim not only of a hit-and-run fugitive but of the law itself. It occurred to her that all the reasoning in the world couldn't thwart this policeman's search. He was clearly determined, and she might well do more harm than good by protesting further. In the legal scheme of things she had nothing to hide. Her purse held no more than the usual feminine paraphernalia. But those books . . . when he ever saw those books . . .

All too soon the squad car drew to a halt on West Cedar Street. Monica was out the door and halfway up her steps before the handsome one caught up. She was too intent on letting herself into the building to hear the cruiser drive off. The few minutes' rest in the car had revived her. It was with remarkable pep—or was it the urge to escape her custodian?—that she trotted up the two flights to her apartment. He reached the landing a single step behind, though, and stood patiently while she unlocked the door.

Once inside, she dropped her purse on the living room sofa, ducked into her bedroom for a split second to toss the bag of books onto a free corner of the open shelving unit, where it might easily be overlooked, and retreated to the bathroom. One look at the face in the mirror caused her to gasp, grow apprehensive, then lean closer toward the mirror.

"It's quite a gash, isn't it?" came the deep voice at the door.

Monica started with fright. "Oh! It's you!" she cried, having somehow expected to be granted this modicum of privacy.

"I thought you might need some help," he returned calmly, studying her bruised temple. She turned back to examine it herself.

"Why didn't you tell me it was this bad?"

"There was nothing you could do about it

there on the sidewalk. Here, let me take a look. Have you got a washcloth?"

Monica knelt to the vanity below the sink, fished out a clean cloth, and handed it to him. "What's your name?" she asked, with perfect spontaneity.

The policeman was silent while he put the cloth under the warm tap, then squeezed out the excess water. "People aren't usually interested in that kind of detail. A cop is a cop." He carefully began to sponge the bruise at her temple.

She gritted her teeth against the soreness. "This one happens to be in my bathroom playing doctor, and I'd like to know what to call him. Acchhh!" She flinched. "Be careful!"

"Hurt?"

"Mmmm."

"I'm sorry. I'm trying to get it clean." He worked on, rinsed the cloth, then continued.

Monica focused on his image in the mirror. "Well?"

He dabbed cautiously. "It doesn't need to be stitched. I would have taken you directly to the hospital if I'd thought it did. Have you got any antiseptic?"

"Your name . . . ?" She could be stubborn herself.

He straightened up and dropped the cloth

into the sink. Then he looked her in the eye. "Michael. Michael Shaw." And he held out a large, lean hand. "The antiseptic, please?"

She stared at him for a minute longer, trying in vain to decipher the coded message in his eyes. The bathroom seemed suddenly very, very small. "Uh . . . I can take care of it," she stammered, tearing her gaze from his, opening the medicine chest, reaching for the spray can, only to have it quickly removed from her fingers.

"Close your eyes," he ordered, and she did. He angled his hand as added protection while he sprayed the cut and the surrounding network of scrapes. Monica gasped at the momentary sting, but it eased instantly.

"Ah. That's better." She breathed more freely when the antiseptic spray had dried. But her relief was short-lived. For Michael Shaw went to work on her shoulder before she could anticipate his move. "I can do that," she protested, to no avail. He held her arm firmly while he repeated the course of treatment on this, the lesser bruise.

It also proved to be the more painful of the two. Monica was increasingly aware of him—the way his fingers easily circled her arm, the way his throat was tanned down the open collar of his shirt, the way she had to look up such a great distance to see his face.

"I take it you live alone," he stated, sparing a second's glance from his work.

"Is this for the record?" she teased softly.

"Would you like it to be?"

"Not particularly. I'd rather the world assumed I had two live-in bodyguards and a growling Doberman."

He finished cleaning her shoulder and reached for the antiseptic. "Have you ever had any trouble?"

"No," she said, "but I hate to invite it." She sucked in her breath when the cold spray hit its mark, then slowly exhaled.

"There you go," he said, replacing the cap of the spray can with a snap. "That should do it."

Monica viewed his handiwork. "Nice job, Shaw. That was above and beyond the call of duty." She met his gaze for an intense moment, then whispered a softer "Thanks."

He too stared for those few seconds as though he were puzzled, before breaking into a slow smile. "My pleasure," he said, tipping an imaginary hat. Only then did she realize that he was indeed without one. His hair was rich and full and sandy brown, finely interwoven with gray threads to lend him an even greater air of dignity. She would never have pegged him for a policeman if it had not been for the uniform.

"Is something wrong?" he asked through the lingering half-smile.

Sensing her imagination was getting out of hand, she broke away from his gaze. "I think I'll get some ice," she murmured and headed for the kitchen.

Several minutes later she emerged, with an ice pack pressed to her temple, to find the kind Officer Shaw in her living room very calmly and deliberately examining the contents of her purse. Annoyed but knowing she couldn't stop him, she crossed to her favorite peacock-backed chair and sank into its comfortable cushions.

"Find anything interesting?" she asked coolly, crossing one leg over the other in an attempt at nonchalance.

"Not yet," he answered, spreading the items out on her coffee table. "Wallet, checkbook, makeup case . . ." He looked up. "I didn't think you were wearing makeup."

"I'm not."

"But you sometimes do?"

"Sometimes." When she was going out socially or to work. For days like today the rule was *au naturel*. She heard the zipper of the makeup case open, then close. "Any other questions?"

"An empty eyeglass case. Why empty?"

Monica's hand flew to the top of her head.

"My sunglasses! Oh, no! They must have fallen off when I was hit!"

He looked up, faintly amused. "What were they doing on your head?"

"Keeping my hair out of my eyes," she offered facetiously. "Besides, the sun wasn't terribly bright *inside* the bookstore." Then she sobered. "It's a shame. They were a terrific pair."

"Prescription?"

"No. Just . . . just . . . terrific." *Designer* would sound pretentious, and it wasn't her habit. "Any chance of finding them?"

He shook his head as he continued to sort through the random assortment of cards and sales slips that had been floating about in her purse. "I doubt it. Someone will have adopted them by now, particularly if they're as terrific as you say." He dangled a set of keys in his hand, a different set from those that had opened her door. "Where to?"

"The building where I work."

"Where's that?"

She took a breath to object but he cast her a stern look and she thought twice. "One-ten Boylston."

"The Harper Building?"

"Uh-huh." This was shaky ground, and she knew what was coming.

"What do you do?"

"I work at the radio station."

"WBKB?"

"That's right. You *are* pretty familiar with Boston." One way to avoid the worst was to change the subject as smoothly and quickly as possible. "How long have you lived here?" There was still that untraceable accent.

She watched Michael shake the purse for anything he may have missed. "Several weeks." He carefully began to replace everything he'd removed.

"Several *weeks*? You can't be a rookie . . ." Shifting more comfortably in the chair, she propped her elbow on the arm and pressed the ice pack back against her head.

He sat back more casually. "Why not?"

She hesitated, wanting to be tactful. "The usual rookie is not much more than a kid. You're a man." The instant she said it she regretted it. It was an understatement.

"You noticed?" He smiled crookedly.

Grateful for the cooling effect of the ice just above her warm cheeks, Monica bid herself stand firm against his appeal. "I couldn't help but notice. You must be slowing down in your old age. You let your buddy do all the running back there."

Those deep brown eyes glinted with humor. "Maybe I chose to be with you. As you said, I am a man."

And I'm a woman, she finished the thought. Much as she was trying to resent his implications, she couldn't. "You're a policeman," she reminded them both. "How old *are* you?" Turning the tables like this, she was in her accustomed role.

Michael indulged her curiosity. "Thirty-eight."

"And you just joined the department?" she asked in surprise.

"Actually I'm visiting."

"Visiting. That's a new one. What does that mean?"

"It means," he replied patiently. "that I'm just on the streets here for the summer."

"Ah. Transferred from another department?" she asked, catching on. He nodded and she probed further. "In the Midwest?"

"Wisconsin."

"Interesting." It was. For all her verbal sparring over the nightly airwaves with and about the police department, she'd never heard of such a thing. But before she could question him further, he stood up and began to wander around her living room. "Uh-oh, the search isn't over yet?" she quipped as he flipped through a batch of magazines that lay on a shelf beside the stereo.

"You were curious. So am I."

Monica had the distinct feeling that the man, rather than the policeman, was the curious one. Again she was aware of the way he dominated the room. And there *was* something about a man in uniform . . .

Disturbed by her thoughts, she squirmed in her chair. "Where's your partner?"

Michael had moved on to the series of small woodcarvings that populated the white mantel. The entire room, the entire apartment, was white, airy, and sunny. The dark figurines stood out clearly. "He's gone for lunch. . . . Did you do these?"

"No . . . You don't eat?"

"I will later. . . . Who carved them? They're good." He'd lifted up Monica's favorite, one of a mother nursing her child. It captured a feeling she'd come to dream of more often lately. There was something devastatingly personal about the way this man's fingers so gently touched the carving.

"A friend," she answered more softly. "He lives in northern Vermont and comes out of seclusion only once a year."

Nodding, Michael carefully replaced the figure, then rounded the sofa and sat down again. Leaning forward with his elbows on his knees and his fingers intertwined, he was "The Thinker" reborn. Monica studied him, wondering what deep thoughts he was thinking, curious even against her will. But he was a policeman.

"Am I under house arrest?" she goaded him quietly.

He looked up and laughed. "Not quite."

"Am I still a prime suspect?"

"You seem pretty clean. I can't quite figure out why you got so defensive back there, though."

"What would *you* have done if you'd been in my place, walking out of a store, being hurled against a wall, then finding yourself on the receiving end of an interrogation?" She paused expectantly. But the only thing she heard was the sound of the doorbell.

Michael was immediately on his feet. "I'll get it. It's Joe."

From her snug perch Monica watched as he quickly located the button to speak to his partner, then buzzed him into the downstairs lobby. He opened her door and disappeared into the hall, only to return seconds later with several bags in his hands . . . but no Joe.

"What *now*?" She heard herself voice her irritation, prompted by the bizarre twist to a day that was supposed to have been so placid.

"Lunch," he announced, crossing right

through to the kitchen, making himself at home.

"Just a minute!" Bolting up from her chair, she followed him into the kitchen. "This is my apartment. I didn't exactly *invite* you here. What do you think you're doing?"

Her indignation was based on principle, but it didn't faze him in the least. "Unwrapping two Italian subs. Now"—he rubbed his hands together and looked around the kitchen—"if you've got some napkins and something cold to drink, we're all set."

"*We?*"

He stopped in his tracks, endearingly unsure. "You'll join me, won't you? I sent poor Joe down to the North End for these. They're the best around. But I can't eat two."

Monica arched a brow. "Is this on the department?"

He met her head-on. "This is on *me.*"

She wanted to ask why but couldn't. "There's a pitcher of iced tea in the fridge. If I'd known you were coming, I'd have stocked a six-pack of beer." She turned to toss her pack of ice into the sink and got down a pair of glasses from the cabinet. When she faced him again, Michael was standing with his hands on his hips.

"I don't drink beer."

"That's a switch," she murmured impulsively.

"Why do you say that?"

She shrugged and set the glasses down on the round butcher-block table. "I don't know. The macho image, I guess." Then feeling suddenly warmer, she flipped on the white Casablanca fan suspended from the ceiling. Its faint hum was a small price to pay for the soothing motion of the air.

"What have you got against the police?" He brought out the iced tea and filled both glasses. She noted his ease and the way his watch gleamed gold against the tanned skin of his wrist. It was a fine watch, no cheap imitation of style.

"Is it that obvious?"

"Well . . . you had nothing to hide from me, but you balked at cooperating."

"No one likes to be manhandled—uh, wrong word." She staunched his protest with her own amendment. "People don't like to be forced into doing things."

"I'm not asking about 'people.' I'm asking about you. What got you so upset?"

"Is this part of your investigation?"

"For the department—no." Left unexpressed was his personal interest.

Monica slid into a chair and reached for

the sandwich Michael offered her. Placing it in front of her on the table, she stared at its jumble of spices and wished that her own thoughts were blander. But the meal suited her well. She was an amalgam of very potent opinions.

With a frown she struggled for the most accurate answer to his question. "Loss of control," she said at last. "I don't like being backed into a corner."

"You had your choice. I remember having given you three," he answered reasonably.

She listened to that deep voice and felt her resentment vanish, to be replaced by a mockery that hit them both. "Why don't I recall having made the choice?"

He paused, then chuckled. "You didn't at that, did you? Did I make the wrong one?"

"Given the alternatives . . . no."

"At least we agree on that," he declared. Biting into his sub, he studied her for a moment, then he let his eye circle the room. "Your place suits you."

"Oh?" She settled back, wondering how observant he was. He still hadn't realized that she'd stashed the bag of books. "Tell me more," she baited him smugly.

"Everything here is open and unadorned. Even you." His eyes led the way. "Carefree hairstyle, no makeup, simple sundress, open sandals—everything unrestrained. You like your freedom, don't you?"

Monica was astonished that he'd hit so close to the mark. "You must be in the wrong field. You've got the instincts of a psychologist."

"Am I right?"

"Close enough." She frowned, genuinely puzzled. "What *are* you doing in the police department? You're totally different from most police officers."

"You've met that many?"

"I've met my share."

Skepticism blended with teasing in his warm, brown gaze. "That's hard to believe . . . a lovely, law-abiding citizen like you . . ."

Her eyes flashed. "Uh-huh. Look what happened to that lovely, law-abiding citizen today. She was all but taken into custody!"

When he tipped his head, she noted the light crease of concern on his brow, and it confused her all the more. Indeed he was different. "That's not exactly true. And what if you'd been seriously hurt? Wouldn't you have wanted us to have been there to get the fastest possible medical attention for you? Or if you'd really been robbed—or mugged—by that fellow we were chasing? Wouldn't you have appreciated our presence then?"

"By all means," she acknowledged gracefully. "But I doubt I would have expected you'd actually catch the fellow."

"That's a negative attitude."

"I'm sorry."

"You really feel that way?"

"Yes."

"Why?"

Monica tempered her glare to a less antagonistic stare, but her prejudices were showing nonetheless. "Because I believe that for most policemen their job is an ego trip. It's not so much the outcome as the dynamics of the chase. It's swaggering around with a gun and a billy club, the ability to give commands and have them obeyed, the right to pull innocent people"—she emphasized the words—"off the street for whatever reason happens to be available. Power. Isn't that the name of the game?"

Michael finished his drink, eyeing her steadily. "Is it?"

Rolling her eyes toward the ceiling, she grimaced. "It's always seemed that way to me."

"Perhaps that's because you're on your own ego trip," he said challengingly, his tone as chilled as the tea he'd just drained. She wondered where his warmth had gone, and half-missed it.

"How can you say that? You don't know anything about me!"

"I know the libber type. She's got a chip on her shoulder against anything that's got both an X and a Y chromosome. Jealousy of the most basic kind."

"That's absurd!" She paused, reflecting. "Actually it's pretty funny. I've never heard *that* one before!"

But Michael wasn't amused. He continued to stare at her. "It's not funny when she won't keep her mouth shut. That kind of woman has to constantly put her man down to make herself look better. She shows up his inadequacies to downplay her own. It's her bid for power. She's threatened."

It sounded as though the handsome Michael Shaw had very definitely been burned at some point in his thirty-eight years. There was a determination in his expression that was indeed threatening. "That's a generalization of the extreme case," she offered less caustically.

"No more of a generalization than yours was . . ."

He had a point but she couldn't quite concede it. It seemed somehow important to maintain a jagged edge between them. She had felt too comfortable with him before.

"It looks like a stalemate, Officer Shaw. You have your preconceptions, I have mine." She stood up and spoke with her greatest air of conviction. Perhaps the time had come to end this adventure. "Now . . . if my privacy isn't too much to ask for . . . you *are* done with your business, I believe, *and* your lunch."

Michael stood in turn, his expression composed, eyes unreadable. "So I'm being turned out?" he asked, the note of quiet humor was unmistakable and unappreciated. It helped her harden herself.

"That's right." She smiled as impersonally as she could. "I trust you'll find some other form of afternoon entertainment." Leaving the kitchen, she crossed through the living room and went directly to the front door, which she opened with a flourish. It was, after all, her turn to hold a bit of that power.

Michael approached, not in the least intimidated. "Did you enjoy your lunch?" As he'd expected, she didn't answer, simply glared. He stepped closer, and she had to tip her head back. She had no idea what he was up to, only knew that there was nothing contrite about him.

"You know, Monica Grant," he began,

more gently than she might have wished, "you're not as modern as you like people to believe."

"What do you mean by that?"

His eyes fell from hers to make the tour of her cheek, her chin, finally resting on her lips. "Your books. You're an old-fashioned girl at heart."

So he'd seen them! She lashed out in anger to cover her embarrassment. "You searched my apartment!" *When?*

"No. Only that bag from the bookstore."

"You had no right!"

"It was my job. Our pickpocket, remember?" he chided her in a deep, smooth voice, knowing she was avoiding the issue, and determined not to let her. "I can almost understand why you were hiding that bag. Not good for the image of the swinging single, the liberated woman at her best?"

"That's a low blow."

"Not low, Monica. Direct." He seemed suddenly intense and very, very close. "I would bet there are times when you'd like to surrender to a man, to let him make the decisions for a change. But somebody out there tells you you've got to be strong and stand on your own two feet, no matter what. Doesn't it get tiring after a while . . . standing all alone?"

His insight shook her to her roots. "And how do you know so much about loneliness and the female mind?"

"Perhaps it's not only the female mind. Loneliness is a universal phenomenon. I know that *I* get tired . . ." His voice trailed off as his expression changed. Suddenly his eyes were warmer in a different way, capturing her, absorbing her, refusing to let her see anything but the man within.

Monica couldn't move. She wanted to yell, to order him from her home, to reclaim the shreds of her dignity, and burrow in solitude. But he understood, he knew.

She even sensed that he was going to kiss her—yet she was helpless to avoid his lips. They touched hers lightly, experimentally, then more firmly and with greater warmth. She felt his heat enter and work its way through her body. Her mind tried to recall who he was, that this was all his power play, his bid for dominance, but it was useless. He was a man whom she found to be extremely attractive, and his challenge was a heady one.

As his mouth moved over hers, gently seeking her response, she felt her resistance begin to crumble. He was tall and strong, a man through and through. Was it wrong to indulge in the moment's pleasure, to pretend that he *was* her hero? Certainly the physical attraction was there, not to mention the inherent clash of outlook that had roughed out many a Chapter One. And if this was reality, as opposed to fiction, she could stop whenever she wanted.

She opened to him slowly, allowing herself to taste the tang of his lips while he brought his hands up to frame her face. She felt dominated yet strangely powerful in her own way as she returned his kiss and felt his shudder. His arms slid around her to press her closer. By reflex she raised her hands to his chest. But rather than the sensual swell of muscle she'd expected, her fingers found a hard metal badge.

Jarred, she pushed back. "Please . . . !" she gasped, and he let her go. In the instant before her hand dropped she felt the rapid beat of his heart.

"It's not that bad . . . once in a while, is it?" he asked gently.

Monica looked away and pressed her fingers to her lips. But Michael captured her chin and tipped her face up until she had no choice but to submit to the fire of his gaze. It danced its way into her once more.

"Maybe what you need is a man to tame you." He spoke more forcefully but with good humor.

"I do not." She enunciated each word, soft and low.

"Isn't that what the swashbuckling hero of your novels would do?" With his arched brow and penetrating gaze, his uniform, gun, and badge and the fine physique beneath it all, he might well have been that hero.

"What I read isn't necessarily what I want."

"Are you so sure?" he asked, his eyes caressing her lips a final time, making her feel all the more defensive.

"Yes!" she exclaimed, but she wasn't sure. There was that element of dream-fantasy in the romances she read. How closely the dream related to her own she wasn't sure. And she wasn't about to discuss it with Michael Shaw.

Sensing her determination, he stepped back and turned to go. "Is your head all right now?"

"Yes."

"Be sure to see a doctor if you feel dizzy or nauseous."

"I'm fine." But she gripped the doorknob behind her for support in the unexpected struggle between desire and frustration. It didn't help when he leaned forward to murmur in her ear.

"Why don't you try *Dreams of Ecstasy* first? It looked pretty good." He started down the steps just in time to avoid being pushed. But he paused at the halfway point. "And, Monica?" She scowled in silent expectancy. "Sorry about the mess on your kitchen table. You'll clean it up like a good girl, won't you?"

If she had had something in her hand, she would have thrown it. As it happened, he had rounded the landing and begun the second flight before she could think of a suitably barbed retort. His footsteps beat a rhythmic tattoo, fading slowly in their descent down the worn wood. It was only when she heard the front door open, then shut that she realized she was still standing on her own threshold. Suddenly giving way to her impotent fury, she kicked the door shut.

Two

Monica stood scowling, marveling at the gall of the man until she had finally calmed down enough to realize he'd done it solely for her benefit. " 'Clean it up like a good girl,' " she mimicked his velvety parting shot. And she headed to the kitchen to do just that—not in obedience but rather out of necessity. Very simply put, there was no one else to do it.

With a fresh glass of iced tea in her hand she returned to the peacock chair to slowly collect her thoughts. Michael had been correct in his evaluation. She liked her freedom. This apartment was indicative of it.

She'd lived here since she first moved from Phoenix four years before. The first thing she'd done was to strip the walls of their dreary wallpaper, the windows of their heavy curtains, and the floors of their ancient carpeting. Then she'd had everything painted white. After intensive sanding and polishing the floor had emerged as solid oak, and beautiful. It had remained unadorned ever since.

Her eye skimmed the room much as Michael Shaw's must have done. High ceilings, tall windows with the sun pouring through, a refreshing breeze wafting by, courtesy of the prized top floor and its cross-ventilating corner location, and furnishings of white Haitian cotton, yellow silk accessories, and clear glass shelves and tables—it was indeed a vision of airiness.

Michael had pegged her perfectly. Still she wondered about his place in the world. He wasn't at all what she would have expected. Even in spite of that last gibe, she couldn't deny the kindness and compassion he'd shown her. And he was obviously intelligent. Strange that he was still pounding a beat, as opposed to moving up in the department hierarchy. Perhaps back in . . . Wisconsin, he'd said . . . he held some other position. What was he doing here? He was so different. . . .

In a moment her thoughts trailed back to that day fourteen years before. She'd been an innocent fifteen year old, young and impressionable, discovering for the first time the price of free expression. The Vietnam War had been in its death throes then, and the last of the peace demonstrations were in progress around the country. Monica had been with her older brother, a veteran himself who'd lost a good friend to the Viet Cong. They'd been quietly sitting with a group outside the local draft board when it was decreed by some faceless higher-up that the demonstration was over.

Still they sat. She remembered being frightened, wanting to leave. But there was the war, the killing, the statement that had to be made. They sat while the police cordon formed. They sat when the dark line advanced. It was only when tempers broke loose and they were bodily removed that the sit-in ended.

Monica shivered the thoughts away. She had survived, as had the other demonstrators. A police record and a dislocated shoulder had been a small price to pay in comparison to that paid by so many young men. As a further legacy of the experience she developed an instinctive and negative response to anything with the initials *PD* on its sleeve.

Michael Shaw wore those initials but had somehow overridden that response. Had it been the depth of his eyes or the gentle touch of his hand? She assumed it had something to do with both. She also suspected it involved much more, but she refused to dwell on that. There were other, more pressing matters to consider. Bounding up from the chair, she put in a call to the station. "Sammy? It's me. Any luck getting Mallory?" Sam Phillips was the producer of the show, and Eugene Mallory was an expert on courtroom tactics at Harvard Law. She wanted him for a program on the insanity defense.

"I just reached him" came the voice at the other end. "He's willing to come in on Friday."

"He *is*?" she exclaimed. "Just like *that*? I thought for sure he'd find some excuse. It was really a shot in the dark!" But a bright light in her day now that he'd consented to be her guest.

A pleased chuckle met her ears. "Shows you're rising in the world, babe. It's becom-

ing the in thing to be on your show. Pretty
soon *they*'ll be calling *us*!"

Monica laughed gaily. "Wouldn't *that*
be something!" Then it was all business
again as she checked her mental calendar.
"Okay. If Mallory's coming on Friday, we'll
have to do some juggling. Matt Morgan will
probably be more flexible than the state rep-
resentative. We can do the segment on main-
streaming the handicapped first thing
Monday."

"Sounds good, Monica. I'll give him a call
now. Are you all set for tonight?"

She glanced at the bulging manila envelope sandwiched between her briefcase
and the wall. "I will be. See you at seven,
Sammy." No sooner had she replaced the receiver than she reached for the material to be
studied. Hers was a three-hour program,
most often divided into two equal segments.
Tonight's A segment was a discussion of auto
insurance practices with the state insurance
commissioner. The B segment belonged to
the author of a book on father-son relationships. In each case she reread the bio of her
guest and skimmed packets of recent clip-
pings that Sammy had put together. In the
case of the author she also skimmed his
book. Then she made a tentative list of ques-

tions to ask before the telephone lines were opened to the public. Her questions were known to be pointed, breaking the ice for her callers and hopefully stirring them up as well. She also had a reputation for sniffing out a potential controversy and opening it up for discussion—consequently those discussions were often heated.

By late afternoon she felt sufficiently knowledgeable to conduct a rousing session. After showering and changing, she looked at her watch. Then she wandered back into the bedroom, where her eye caught the bag of books she'd stowed there this morning. He had indeed found them. The books were stacked in a double pile on top of the bag, with *Dreams of Ecstasy* smack on top.

When had he gone through her bedroom? Or had he simply spotted the bag and only searched it? It had to have been those few moments after he'd cleaned her bruises, when she'd gone to the kitchen in search of ice. What else had he seen here?

This room too was true to Monica. It continued the white-and-yellow motif from the rest of the apartment, expressing it with a flowered quilt and matching sheets, the thinnest wisp of a gauze drape, a white bamboo headboard and companion dresser.

A huge mirror above the dresser gave the illusion of a room beyond, it too bright and spacious.

What might an observant Michael Shaw learn here? He might learn that there was a definite feminine flair to the woman, from the dust ruffles below the quilt to the tray of delicately shaped perfume bottles. He might learn that she'd come from a large family, if he chose to study the framed photograph on the dresser that pictured her parents, three brothers, two sisters, and their assorted children. Monica smiled as she studied the photo herself. It had been taken last Thanksgiving at the family home in Cleveland. What a wonderful time that had been! She *liked* her family, more than many could claim to. Each of her siblings was an interesting character, not to mention her parents, whose nonconformity had inspired the lot of them. Family gatherings at the Grant home were truly happenings.

She turned to face the large bookshelf unit, bamboo painted white also with glass shelves. If anything was revealing, it was the contents of this piece, the books she'd accumulated over the past four years—both for work and pleasure. There were biographies and works of non-fiction, psychological studies and thrillers. All were autographed by the authors, who had appeared on her show at one time or another. And then there was her collection of love stories, set on its own shelves, unautographed, purely for her enjoyment. Had Michael Shaw studied these titles? If so, he'd really had a field day!

Her eye fell on the new books. *Dreams of Ecstasy*. It did look like a good one. Should she start it now? No, she thought, she'd be better to review her thoughts for the evening's show. But . . . what about one chapter? A half-hour's worth? Surely she could spare that. But then, the argument went, she'd have to tear herself away from the plot when the going was apt to be getting good. Far better to wait until tonight, when she might have at least an hour at a stretch to read.

She reached for the book. So much for her better judgment. Her morning had been trying enough to merit this small reward. Just a chapter . . . she'd even set the timer to remind herself that she was due at the studio at seven.

Stretched comfortably on the sofa with her bare feet propped on the coffee table, she opened the book and began to read. Within minutes she was transported back in time to Regency England, where her family was at the heart of society and she was its budding flower. She was young and beautiful, poised but with a temper to match her wild amber eyes. And she was being forced into a marriage she didn't want.

Somewhere in the shadows was a man. She didn't know his name, or for that matter his reason for hovering on the edge of society. He seemed to know the people that one had to know. And he moved about at will, apparently accepted by those around him. There was something in his face, though, something dark and mysterious. And she found him to be very, very handsome.

The buzzer sounded, and Monica jumped. Time already? With a frown she marked the page and set the book on her bed. She'd read more tonight when she returned. Then, as she dressed, she pondered her love of romance. Was she really an old-fashioned girl at heart, as Michael Shaw had suggested? Did she want a man to "tame" her? Or did she simply crave that very special loving of the man-woman kind?

She'd been in love once. With Allan. They'd lived together in Phoenix for nearly two years. The first year had been wonderful, a blissful novelty for them both. The second year, however, had been different. Somehow, slowly, they'd drifted apart, finding new friends and alternate plans. When they'd finally agreed to split up, it had been a mutual decision. There were neither hard feelings nor regrets. Monica assumed she hadn't loved him all that much after all.

There were memories though. Beautiful ones at that. She had felt a sense of companionship, had glimpsed the pleasure of oneness with a man. During that first year she and Allan had been tuned in to one another on every wavelength. It had been a lovely feeling.

Was it that experience that had sparked her leaning toward romance? Or did it all stem from something else, something deeper? She'd had many a date since she'd arrived on the Boston scene, yet none had stirred her as her heroines were stirred by their heroes.

In honest analysis, she saw herself as a strong woman, willful in her way and independent. In a similarly realistic admission she knew she'd someday want a man to match that strength, a man she could lean on when she felt the need, a man whom she couldn't intimidate, a man like ... like ... Michael Shaw ... ?

Muttering an angry epithet, she thrust her feet into her sandals, grabbed up her purse, briefcase, and that stuffed manila envelope, and headed for work. She stopped along the way on Charles Street for a quick supper, crossed the Common through the light early-evening foot traffic, and entered the Harper Building right on time. No one had recognized her—the beauty of being a faceless voice on the radio waves. An hour later though, thousands of ears were tuned when the news ended and her smoothly melodious voice flowed out through Boston and vicinity.

"Good evening," she began with her standard greeting, "and welcome to *Speaking Out*. This is Monica Winslow and it's my pleasure to introduce my first guest, the Insurance Commissioner for the Commonwealth, Randolph Post. Mr. Post was appointed by the governor eighteen months ago after his predecessor was forced to resign in response to allegations of a widespread kickback scheme. Mr. Post"—she slid a microphone closer to her guest—"perhaps you could begin by telling us what has happened on the commission under your administration . . ."

The show ran its course, from eight to eleven. Walking home afterward, Monica reflected on it, seeing its higher points and its lower points and learning from each. But when the door to her apartment had finally shut tight behind her, she didn't want to think about work. Rather, she changed into a cool cotton nightgown, propped the pillows behind her in bed, and picked up her book.

She awoke the next morning, brimming with resolve. By ten o'clock she was sitting in the chair of her Newbury Street hairdresser, staring alternately at his reflection and her own in the mirror.

She issued a soft command. "Okay, Robert. Do it."

Robert eyed her blankly. "Do what, M.G.?" No one else called her by her initials. He had thought it funny at first, then claimed that the pun fit her. Classy, he said, and she was flattered.

"Layer the front."

"Bangs? You're kidding! I've been trying to get you to do that for months. What's brought about the turnaround?" He came from behind to face her directly and squinted at her forehead. "Where *did* you get that bruise?"

She'd been asked the same question last night at work. Then as now, she passed off the incident with a laugh. "I walked into a wall."

"Try again. Monica Grant doesn't walk into walls. She sees *everything*."

"Not quite," she said sheepishly. "I was walking along Washington Street yesterday and this fellow accidentally barged into me." She shrugged at the outward simplicity of it. "I ricocheted off the wall."

"Hmm. Must've looked worse yesterday."

She grinned. "It did. The swelling's gone down now. It's really nothing."

"But you want to cover it up." He moved behind her once again, as though all business talk had to be conducted through the mirror.

"That's as good an excuse as any."

Robert took a deep breath, put both hands on her shoulders, and sighed with resignation. "If that's the only one you can find, I guess it'll have to do. I've been telling you all along that it would soften your look, add a little wispiness." He made an illustrative gesture with his fingers. "Romance is *in* . . . or haven't you heard?"

She didn't give him an answer, simply pointed her own finger at her head. "*Do* it . . . before I change my mind . . ." Then she laughed as Robert instantly reached for his scissors.

*   *   *

The doorbell rang that afternoon while Monica was wallowing in a treatise on tax planning written by her scheduled guest for the evening's segment A. Her material was strewn all over the kitchen table. She quite happily left it to answer the door.

"Yes?" she called through the intercom.

The answering voice was slightly distorted, hindering immediate recognition.

"I've got your sunglasses."

Sunglasses? But she'd lost them . . . and there was certainly no identification on them. Only one man knew that they were lost. "Shaw? Is that you?"

"Can I come up?"

She pressed the buzzer without a second thought. She opened the door, went out into the hall, and leaned over the railing to watch the dark-clad figure come into view. It was a rare treat. He carried himself well, with that air of confidence that gave him an edge. Looking tall and doubly lean in that near-black uniform of his, he took the stairs easily, slowing down only for the last few steps. Monica felt strangely excited.

"I hope I'm not disturbing anything." He peered around her toward her apartment. "I thought you might be able to use these."

Maddening, she mused, that she was the only one left breathless by his climb! "You found them! I thought they were gone for good!" She reached for the glasses and inspected them for scratches.

"Your friend in the bookstore saw them lying by the curb soon after we left. When I went back to ask, he had them put away for you."

Catching the glitter of amusement in his eyes, Monica sensed that his thoughts were dwelling on the books she'd bought rather than on the "friend" she'd bought them from. But she refused to get defensive. "I appreciate your going back. You didn't have to do that."

"I had to go back that way anyway." Again he looked past her. "May I . . . come in?"

"Uh . . . is this business or pleasure?" she asked, even as she wondered if it would matter. But he smiled, and she knew it did, though in a far different way than she might have expected a day ago. Much as she wished it was simply the diversion from tax planning that she welcomed, she had to admit that she was actually glad to see him.

When he smiled and said, "A little of both," she had no choice.

With a deceptively carefree toss of her head toward her living room, she made the invitation official. "Please. Come in."

Michael preceded her but stood in the living room when she continued on toward her bedroom. Returning immediately, she held out his handkerchief, now freshly washed and folded neatly.

"A gift for a gift. Thank you."

"Thank *you*," he replied, tucking the cloth into a back pocket. "Do you have a few minutes?"

"I think I can manage to make them. What can I do for you?" *How's that for taking the offensive?* she complimented herself. But her smugness vanished with a quick intake of breath at his next words.

"You can tell me how you're feeling, for one thing."

"Fine. I'm really fine."

"No problem with your head?" He looked toward the fast-fading bruise.

"No more than the usual scrambled brains," she quipped, but he was staring more intently. "Is something wrong?"

"You look different."

"Ahah! So you finally noticed! Typical of a man," she half-murmured to herself. But he recovered quickly and grinned victoriously.

"It's your hair. You had it cut."

"Just the front."

"It looks great! Really pretty. Softer.

More . . . more . . ." He seemed to hesitate for a minute before deciding to take the risk. "More feminine."

"Is that a compliment?"

His eyes warmed by degrees. "I'd say so. A man likes his woman to be soft and feminine at times."

"Only at times?" she rejoined, feeling utterly soft and feminine before him.

"Only at times." His voice was low, verging on husky. "When they're alone, and she curls up against him, warm and pliant—"

"How can you ever be a policeman?" she cried, desperately needing to break the spell he cast. "You've got to be a dreamer, a poet."

"It's not possible to be both?"

"Cop and poet?" She wandered over to the sofa and sat down. "I doubt it. The policeman's lot is one of hard-boiled realism, isn't it? You'd know better than I."

Following her gesture, Michael took the armchair opposite her. "Not necessarily. Perhaps that's what I'm doing here."

"In my apartment?"

"In Boston."

"What *are* you doing in the city? You never quite explained that to me."

He seemed suddenly to be more cautious.

"My . . . boss . . . felt it might be a good idea for me to observe the workings of a department larger than my own. I might pick up some things . . ."

"Well . . . have you?"

"Uh-huh." He grinned that crooked grin of his, and she sensed he was on firmer footing. She also sensed he'd change the subject. "Your sunglasses."

"No luck with the pickpocket?"

When he shook his head, a swathe of sandy-gray hair fell down over his brow. "We're working on it."

"What did he take that drew your attention to him in the first place?"

"A gold bracelet. You know, the type women dangle loosely on a wrist?" Monica thought she was hearing the beginnings of the typically chauvinistic you-provoked-it-therefore-it's-your-fault argument, but Michael went on with surprising sympathy. "This particular wrist was that of a frail sixty-eight year old." He shook his head in amazement. "God bless her, for a little lady she made a whale of a racket."

Monica couldn't resist the barb. "Who was she angrier at—the thief for lifting her bracelet . . . or you for losing him?" But where there once might have been disdain in her tone, there was only a hint of teasing.

Michael responded in kind, with one eyebrow roguishly raised. "Next time I'll let you lie bleeding in the gutter."

"I wasn't hurt that badly," she drawled, but he only grimaced his disagreement. "Anyway"—she cleared her throat, feeling particularly vulnerable—"what's the business that brought you here today?" She was really wondering about the pleasure end of it but didn't have the courage to ask.

He grew serious, his jaw tightening. "I wondered if you might have remembered something now that the initial shock has worn off. I hate to pester you, but we do need a description."

"Couldn't the woman who was robbed tell you anything?"

"She saw the back of his head when she realized that her bracelet was missing. He took off like a bullet once she began to yell."

Monica's lips thinned. "I don't remember anything about him. He must have been pretty big to have knocked me over with such force."

"We know that he's roughly five-ten or five-eleven, maybe a hundred and eighty pounds. But we've got nothing on his coloring other than dark hair. What we need is something on his features. A distinguishing characteristic. Anything."

She knitted her brows in concentration, struggling to recreate the scene in her mind's eye. "I remember leaving the bookstore, coming out into the heat of the street, turning, starting to walk . . . then being hit. I must have had my eyes down against the glare."

"Why didn't you just put on your sunglasses?"

"I may have been reaching for them at the time. I can't remember."

"Do you remember looking toward him at all? It'd be a natural instinct to try to see what hit you."

She looked up sharply. "Not when you're half-dazed! The first clear thing I remember was hearing your voice." And what a voice it was. She'd never forget its smooth, calming lilt.

Without her realizing it, her gaze had softened. Against her will it dropped to his lips, her thoughts no longer on his voice. Instead, she recalled how he'd kissed her yesterday.

She should have been furious. That kiss had been expressive of male dominance.

She'd been vulnerable then, and he'd taken advantage of her. But, no . . . there had been something in his kiss that had taken it beyond pure lust. She had enjoyed it, had returned it. Just as now a part of her wanted to feel those lips again . . .

"Monica!" She jumped at the harshness in his tone, the sudden flare of anger in his eyes. "Try to remember!"

That was what she'd been doing, though not of the right event. Confused by his impatience, she frowned. "I'm trying. But I can't give you anything."

He stared at her for several pulse-revving seconds. Then he glanced at his watch. "When do you work, anyway?"

"Evenings."

"What do you do?"

"I told you. I work at WBKB."

"I know that. But what do you do there?"

This was the tricky part. "Oh, you know." She waved a hand, gesturing away the insignificance of her position. "Every station has its team. I'm one of the bunch."

But Michael was one of another bunch, and his team asked questions. They also slitted their eyes and made one feel very, very guilty. "Why do I get the feeling that you're evading the issue? Are you hiding something?"

She returned his narrowed gaze, fighting fire with fire. "This isn't the first time you've asked me that question." If he had run a check, he would have known about her skirmishes with the police, both past and present. Evidently he hadn't seen fit to investigate. It was at once gratifying . . . and disappointing. But she propped her chin on her fist and forced a smile, opting for nonchalance. "What do *you* think I'm hiding?"

Michael leaned forward also, elbows on his thighs, one fist tucked inside the cupped fingers of his other hand. As he shrugged his eyes skimmed the length of her bare legs, her shorts, and her shirt, coming to rest with nerve-tingling inevitability on the gentle swell of her breasts. It was all she could do to sit still. When he looked at her that way, she wanted to melt.

"I really don't know," he countered, then paused. "Do you work every night?"

"Monday through Friday." This was Wednesday.

"Then you've got to work tonight?"

"Uh-huh. Why?" She'd gone through this same routine with many a man. Was he actually going to ask her out? The thought of that terrified her. What would she ever say?

But her fears were unfounded—on that score at least. "I'd like you to come down to the station with me."

A whole new gamut of worries erupted. "The station?" Her eyes widened in horror. "What for?"

"Relax. You're not under arrest." He was joking, but she'd temporarily lost her taste for humor.

"Then why should I go to the station?" The pitch of her voice rose as she sat up straight. There was bound to be someone who'd recognize her, and she'd never hear the end of it. For some reason she didn't want Michael Shaw to know that she and her show had been a major thorn in the side of the police department for months and months.

If Michael thought her reaction to be out of proportion, he chose to be patient. "I'd like you to go through some picture books. Mug shots. Something may strike a chord."

"But I've told you that I can't remember anything."

"There's always the possibility of subliminal recognition, Monica." Again the calming tone. "You may see a picture—the right picture—and it'll ring a bell."

"What if I hit a wrong picture and dredge up some other face I may have seen on the streets? Then you fellas would haul in some innocent man—"

"None of the men in those books are angels. They wouldn't be there if they were. And I wouldn't haul anybody in without checking it out first. If you picked out a red-headed midget, we'd obviously know it was a mistake. We also have several leads about this fellow . . . if he's the notorious pickpocket."

"Leads?" she exclaimed, falling victim to predisposition. "That's a good one. Leads for the BPD are usually in inverse proportion to corruption."

Michael was perfectly still. "You sound very convinced."

"It's common knowledge. The department is rife with corruption."

"And on what do you base that judgment?" he asked quietly.

"Come on, Shaw! It's all over the papers. Your innocence can be forgiven since you're new here, but I'm sure Boston isn't unique. Don't tell me that they're all totally upstanding blue knights back there in Wisconsin."

"Every department has its problems. That doesn't mean the department is useless."

"Maybe not useless. Certainly crippled. Have you any idea how much pot has 'disappeared' from police custody within the last six months?"

He didn't blink. "You're talking about the state police, one particular heist, and the total was a cool $1.5 million. Thefts from local districts have been a small fraction of that."

"You've done your homework," she replied dryly. "But tell me about Boston. What percentage of last year's homicides have been solved?"

"Roughly sixty percent."

"And robberies?"

"That's a broad term."

"Okay. Narrow it down to burglaries. Private citizens' homes . . . like this one. How many of those cases have been solved?"

He held her gaze steadily. "Less. Perhaps thirty percent."

"And that's not to mention retrieving the goods. Chop the percentage in half! Fifteen percent. Now that's poor!"

"And you think it doesn't bother us?" he asked, his voice showing tension at last.

"Does it? I often wonder. All it takes is for one spectacular case to be solved, and the public puts you right back up there on that pedestal."

"Not you?"

"Not me."

"Why, Monica?" he asked, standing up, slowly beginning to pace in a way that reminded her of a dark, sleek panther circling his prey. Monica wondered if she'd let her temper go too far. "Why are you so down on us? There has to be something personal behind your dislike."

"I'm realistic, that's all. I read the papers, I see what's happening all around me. And I have to ask myself if half of the squad is spending its time like you are now—" She cut off the thought herself, knowing that this time she *had* gone too far. She sat and waited, staring at her hands, sensing when Michael moved around the room and came to stand behind her.

Propping his hands on the back of the sofa, he leaned forward until his lips were a whisper from her ear. "Do you know what they say about airport duty?" She couldn't even shake her head, he was that close. "It's wrecked many a good marriage. Policemen often ask to be taken off it. And do you know why?" His breath fanned her ear, and she knew he could actually feel the rapid beat of her heart. "Because the men assigned to airport duty receive on the average four propositions a night. Propositions. Women approach them, turned on by the uniform, the badge, the gun. Lonely women. Women in Boston just for the night."

"There *is* something about a man in uniform." She spoke her earlier thoughts aloud and was instantly appalled. To make matters worse, his mouth at her ear began to nibble on the soft lobe and she felt her chest constrict. But she couldn't move . . . or protest. "You could always . . . refuse . . ." she suggested softly.

His lips touched her neck, and she offered it to him instinctively. "We're human," he whispered in return. "Men. Not supermen. When a woman sits as sweetly and invitingly as you are—"

"I am not!" From somewhere she found the strength to pull away. "And I didn't ask you to come here today." She leaned forward, her head in her hands, not daring to look around at Michael. He would surely be able to see how much he had affected her.

For what seemed an eternity there was nothing but silence. Finally he spoke. "Shall we go?"

She had hoped he'd given up on that tack. When she chanced a glance over her shoulder, she saw him waiting, hands on hips, his expression veiled behind the badge. "Must I?"

"I can't force you, Monica. But if it's hypocrisy you're after, I'd suggest you begin at home. It's one thing to criticize us for our dubious apprehension rate. It's another thing to accept that part of our problem is the reluctance of the average citizen to cooperate with our investigations. Those same citizens who criticize us the loudest are often the first to shy away from involvement . . . in this case"—his gaze hardened in accusation—"simply spending an hour or two looking through some books at the station."

His point hit home. Despite her deepseated reservations his reasoning was solid. She had no choice but to acquiesce. "I'll be right with you," she murmured, rising and rounding the sofa to head for the bedroom. "I'd better change."

"What you're wearing is fine," he called after her, but she turned on him then in frustration, her fists clenched at her sides.

"I'm *not* one of those lonely women looking for a playmate. And since you've just shown me how, uh, human *you* are, I think I'll be safe in something more . . . discreet."

Her cinnamon hair made a circling arc behind her as she twirled around and fled to the privacy of her room. When she returned, she was wearing a pair of sedate white slacks, a short-sleeved burgundy blouson jersey, and her sunglasses, hoping against hope that she'd go unrecognized.

"Ready?" Michael asked more solicitously.

She faced him pertly. "My car or yours?" she quipped, then passed him and led the way downstairs, knowing the answer already. Nothing was going to be easy where Michael Shaw was involved. Nothing!

Three

To Monica, it was as if the entire world was staring when Michael escorted her up the broad stone steps and into the police station. She felt exposed and vulnerable, then positively entombed when the large door swung shut behind them, excluding both sunshine and fresh air.

"This way," he said softly. Then, sensing her discomfort, he put a light hand at the back of her waist. She drew reassurance from it.

They passed the front desk and climbed another stairway, this one narrower, actually snug when they chanced to encounter two-way traffic. She tried to look as inconspicuous as possible, yet even her low-heeled white sandals seemed to strike a deafening beat on the floor. She felt foreign, out of place here, a detainee in the enemy camp. Again the past crowded in on her, and she wished she were anyplace else.

"You okay?" Michael asked in gentle reminder of his presence. Once more she was comforted.

"Uh-huh." She nodded.

"You look scared to death. It's really no big thing, you know, looking through the books."

"I know."

He leaned closer as they rounded a corner and headed down another corridor. "The sun's gone in. You can take the glasses off if you want."

She heard his teasing and decided to emulate it. "They're my disguise. I'm doing this strictly incognito . . . or hadn't you guessed?"

"Oh, I guessed, all right. You must have quite some past to hide."

"You never know," she murmured with a slanted smile then steeled herself as she was guided into the squad room. In her peripheral vision she could see desks and chairs, open railings dividing each cubicle, plus an array of personnel wearing the same dark uniform as Michael. There were others there too, victims, witnesses, even perhaps a suspect or two, each sitting beside his respective inquisitor. And there was the low din of voices, echoing eerily from the high ceilings, rising with intermittent emotion, then falling off again.

Michael led her to one desk in a corner of the room, far enough from the door to have made the walk tedious but at least affording a bit of privacy. She took the seat he offered.

"I'll be right there," he said. Then he squeezed her shoulder. "Don't go away."

She cast him a vengeful stare before he turned and walked off, presumably to fetch the mug books for her. She couldn't help but note how majestic he seemed in this dingy place. Daring to glance at the others in the room now, she marveled again at how different Michael was. There was also small solace in the fact that no one appeared to have noticed their entrance, each evidently embroiled in his own personal calamity.

Police stations were indeed receptacles of misfortune. At one desk was an elderly gentleman, his face buried in his hands as he tried to accept that he'd been robbed at gunpoint two hours before. At another was a young woman, a mother, sadly overweight and pitifully dressed, giving the officer at hand a description of her son, who'd been missing for two days. At a third sat a drunk, slouched in a quiet stupor. Yet a fourth was the temporary way station of a woman in rags, one of the "bag people" roaming the inner city. She was the most vocal of the group, wailing periodically to protest her displacement from what she had thought to be a prime alley.

The scene in the squad room was a sad reminder of reality, but Michael's reappearance eased the gloom. Monica followed his progress, feeling her spirits lift as he drew near.

"I could almost imagine that you missed me," he kidded her as he dropped several oversized notebooks with a thud onto the desk.

She drew into herself. "This place is chilling."

"You've never been in a squad room before?" This remark, which was phrased so casually, had a definite edge, which she proceeded to ignore just as pointedly.

"Not like this." She glanced around again. "Does it ever bother you?"

"What? This?" His gaze followed hers, then returned. "Of course it does. It bothers me every time I'm here. It's discouraging to see this amount of sadness in the world . . . and ours is only a very small pocket."

Both were silent for a minute, Michael reflecting on that sadness, Monica admiring that reflection. His sensitivity was another thing to his credit.

"Here." He broke their silence to point to his chair. "You sit here behind the desk. It'll be more comfortable for you." Monica did as he suggested. Perching on the corner of the desk, he flipped open the first of the books. "Just take your time and go through each page. Tell me if anything clicks."

Dutifully she began to look through the shots, turning one page, then the next. After a bit Michael took over, flipping each page when her headshake signaled failure. If she'd found the squad room to be a discouraging sight, the pictures before her were as bad. Granted, mug shots were notoriously poor portraits, but Monica had never confronted as angry, as surly a crew in her life.

"*La crème de la crème,*" she cracked nervously.

Michael's facetious rejoinder seconded the thought. "Many of them are quite well respected in their fields."

"So I'm told." She'd had a guest on the show once, an ex-convict who had written about just this phenomenon. Status among criminals. It was depressing, to say the least.

Page after page she studied the faces. Nothing. She was marginally aware of the squad room activity, policemen, police-women coming and going. Occasionally the renewed wails of the bag lady drew her head up in alarm. But everything was under control, and Michael was steadfast, right beside her.

As the minutes went by it grew harder not to look for diversion. And the diversion was there—in the taut stretch of dark trousers across a solid thigh, in the manly sprinkling of hair over the back of the hand that turned the pages one by one, even in the clean scent of him as he leaned over her shoulder, a scent that contrasted so sharply with the musty, stale smell of the station. She needed some other diversion.

"This is really no good!" she exclaimed in frustration. "I don't recognize anything. They're all beginning to look the same to me."

"Okay." Michael straightened up. "Let's take a break. Coffee?"

"Mmmm. That would be nice."

"Come on." He gestured for her to stand up, and she was momentarily taken aback, somehow expecting that he'd bring the coffee to her at his desk. Walking back through the squad room again wasn't her first choice of a break, but the coffee at the end of the tunnel? She could use it.

The trek was uneventful enough. Several heads turned when they passed, but there were no reactions other than nods to Michael. For her part, Monica was sure she didn't recognize anyone. Nonetheless she was relieved when she found herself being ushered into a smaller side room, a more private office containing, most importantly, a percolator, packets of tea, instant coffee, sugar, powdered cream, and a beckoning stack of styrofoam cups. It also contained a man in a suit behind a desk. She assumed he was a detective.

"How's it goin', John?" Michael acknowledged the man's presence briefly, not waiting for an answer before turning back to Monica. "How do you take it?" he asked, proceeding to fill a cup with hot water pending her further command.

"Black is fine." She watched while he opened one small envelope, poured its contents into the steaming water, and stirred it. Then he handed it to her.

"Sorry it's not fresh brewed."

"No problem."

"Hey, Shaw!" A head poked through the doorway. "Have you got the Danielson file?"

Michael paused and frowned. "Try Smith's desk. I gave it to him this morning."

"Sure thing." His fellow officer let a hand linger on the door-jamb, then was gone.

"You want this room, Mike?" This from the poker-faced detective at the desk.

"No, thanks, John. We're going in here." He cocked his head toward another door off the first office, finished stirring his coffee, then took Monica's elbow and guided her through to an even more private room, this one deserted. When the door closed to shut out the rest of the station, she breathed a sigh of relief. Without a word she walked around to the window and stared out.

An hour in a police station was a sobering experience, if not a downright depressing one. Michael Shaw's presence was its only saving grace. And that fact was as sobering in its own way. The cycle began again.

"You're very quiet." That deep voice pierced her thoughts. She simply glanced up at him then sipped her coffee as she returned her sights to the street below. "It's a switch," he went on. "You've usually got an answer for everything." She shrugged, still silent. "This place really bothers you, doesn't it?"

She inhaled deeply, then slowly released the breath with a soft, whispered "Yes."

Michael leaned against the wall by the window so that he could see her face. "Would you tell me why?"

She removed her sunglasses, propped them on top her head, and looked at him warily. But there was no hint of interrogation in his tone, simply curiosity, personal interest. She frowned down at her coffee. "It's really not a secret," she began. "You could find out easily enough anyway."

When she faltered, he coaxed her on. "I'm listening."

Her manner was subdued as she related the story of that initial run-in with the law fourteen years before. For the first time though, her anger was easily tempered, as though this present experience had been an emotional release.

"So," she concluded, "if you'd checked up on me, you'd have discovered that I have a police record myself."

He had taken it all in stride and now spoke in that same calm voice. "I don't know as I'd call that a record."

"It's in writing."

"Perhaps. Is *that* what bothers you?" he asked, rightfully puzzled.

"The record per se? No. The experience?

Yes. Police and police stations evoke this kind of gut response in me. I can't help but feel uneasy here." She'd still only told him half of the story. The past was past. Somehow she'd known he would understand. But the present, her job, her reputation as a critic of the department—he might well have more trouble with that.

She looked up in time to catch the warming glow in his eyes. "It's certainly not the greatest place in the world. I think we'd all rather be somewhere else. But places like this are a necessity. The law may have its faults, but it's still critical to the survival of our society."

"Now you sound like a lawyer." She smiled, almost shyly.

Michael shot her an unfathomable glance. "Would you rather I was a lawyer?"

It was an interesting question. From the start Monica had felt attracted to him. From the start—was that really only yesterday? Moreover, the attraction had persisted despite the badge he wore and all that it represented. What if he *had* been a lawyer and there had been nothing at all to stand between them? What then? It was a situation she was reluctant to consider. For there was something threatening about the force of that attraction, something threatening to the independent life-style she'd established. Threatening . . . but still tempting. There was that element of fantasy, of romance she craved.

"Why did you become a cop?" she asked, steering back onto safer ground.

He grinned endearingly. "Doesn't every little boy want to grow up to be one?"

"Most don't actually make it. They outgrow the urge, along with blocks and teddy bears."

"Blocks are for building, teddy bears for cuddling. When one finds a more grown-up substitute, the original gets left behind. I discovered pine two-by-fours when I was twelve, women when I was somewhere around sixteen."

" 'Somewhere?' " A teasing smile tickled her lips. "I thought every man could pin down his first conquest to the year, month, and day, if not the hour."

He mirrored her smile. "I didn't think you'd be interested in the details. Of course, if you'd like, I can give you a blow by blow—"

"That won't be necessary. Just tell me about that other urge—the one to grow up to be a policeman."

"I outgrew it."

"Ah, that makes sense," she replied facetiously. "Now tell me that you're a journalist studying the local good guys for a piece you hope to write. Perhaps even a screenplay."

"Not exactly." He lounged back more comfortably against the wall, as if settling in for a lengthy bout.

"Then what *are* you doing here in that getup?"

"Precisely what I told you yesterday. I'm here on leave from my own department to get to know the workings of the BPD."

"Okay," she conceded more quietly. "Then we get back to my original question. Why a cop? If you outgrew the urge at some point—by the way, what point was that? I mean, you've already told me about blocks and teddy bears."

"I outgrew the urge to be a policeman when I was nine."

"What happened then?"

He didn't hesitate, apparently surer than she was about the past. "I witnessed a police chase in which a cruiser lost control and hit another child on the sidewalk not terribly far from where I stood."

Monica was horrified. "How awful!" She faltered. "Was the child killed?"

"No. He wasn't killed, just badly hurt. He recovered nicely, no permanent damage done. To me, though, it was the destruction of the myth that the policeman can do no wrong."

She could see the fire in his eyes and knew that his experience had been as grave to him as her own had been to her. Most people had a story to tell, an event that had shaken their lives more than others, she mused. Yet the vital link was still missing in Michael's case.

"What brought you back to the fold, so to speak?" she asked gently.

Michael took a deep breath and stood away from the wall. He swirled the coffee around in his cup, drained the dregs, then crushed the styrofoam in his hand and tossed it in a nearby basket. "Many of the same things that have bothered you began to bother me." Still there was the fire in his eyes, defensive in its way.

"Like . . . ?"

". . . lack of effectiveness and understanding, incompetence, yes, corruption . . ."

"So you're working for change from the inside?"

"That's right."

"And you think you can make a difference?"

"I can sure as hell try!"

"As a patrolman on the beat?"

"That's where I am for the summer."

"And then where?"

She couldn't help but sense a secret in his smile. "Who knows?"

"Now wait a minute," she argued, only half jokingly. "If you were eighteen I might buy that line. But you're no beginner."

His lips quirked at the corners. "I believe we've established that already, haven't we?"

"Yes," she conceded quickly, well remembering that earlier discussion and the demonstration that followed it. Then she forced herself to remain composed as she turned to watch him settle against the edge of the table. This time it was she who had her back to the window and Michael's face that was more fully lit. She was struck once more by its depth, the knowing eyes, the determined lips, the beginnings of a five o'clock shadow on his square, manly jaw.

Monica had to struggle to pick up the train of thought she'd momentarily lost. "But . . . can a man your age really afford a *who knows?*"

He grinned again. "Why not?"

She groaned softly. "Unnh. One answer as bad as the next."

"Seriously, is it ever too late for a person to try something new? And isn't the desire to improve on the old one of the most basic motivating forces in life?"

"No . . . and yes. It's just surprising, that's all."

He eyed her more cautiously. "How so?"

Tossing back her head, she gathered her hair together at her nape and lifted it from her neck for a moment's coolness. It was an unconscious nervous gesture. "I somehow might have thought you to be a family man. You know, house, wife, children. For that kind of man a *who knows* is dangerous."

She'd barely finished her speech when Michael leaned forward. His hand snaked out to snag her waist and draw her to him. Her thighs were imprisoned by his before she could begin to react to the assault. "If I was that kind of man, I wouldn't have kissed you yesterday," he drawled. "You know that." His wrists had crossed at the back of her waist and his fingers rested recklessly lower.

She did know it, though she had no idea how. Yet when he'd kissed her yesterday, she'd safely assumed him to be free. Now she felt his nearness, and her senses cried for more. But she put her hands on his forearms and applied token pressure. There was no give at all in his sinewed flesh.

"Michael . . . please! What if someone walked through that door right now?"

"Do you know that that's the first time you've used my first name. Say it again."

"This is ridiculous, Michael—"

"There! Mmmm. It sounds nice. More personal than my last name."

He had a point, as did she. "Please . . . this isn't exactly a personal situation—"

His fingers applied a hint of pressure to the small of her back. "I'd say it's getting there fast."

"This is a *police* station!"

He chuckled. "I know that." Then he pulled her a little closer, and she found her hands at his shoulders. "Tell me, would you scream if I kissed you?"

"And risk getting your buddies in here? They'd probably claim I was asking for it."

"You could be right there."

"I haven't asked for a thing!" she protested.

"I meant that you were right in your assumption about my, uh, colleagues. They probably would blame you. But you haven't answered my question. Would you scream if I kissed you?"

An absurd thought, but she couldn't quite deny it as bluntly. "This isn't the most romantic of spots . . ." Even now, she knew it didn't matter. Already her awareness of her surroundings had begun to fade; the only thing left in her consciousness was Michael.

"Would you?" he pressed, his gaze narrowed with good humor.

"What if someone did walk in?" Her luck had held. No one had recognized her yet. But if she should be found in Michael Shaw's arms by someone she knew, she'd never live it down.

"They'd knock first. Besides, John is on guard out there. So . . . what'll it be? Would you fight me?"

Monica shrugged, eyeing him helplessly. When he proceeded to squeeze her tightly, she caught her breath. It seemed she could feel every inch of his long, hard body.

"Would you?"

"No," she whispered, then tipped her head back to welcome his lips as they met hers. It seemed an eternity since he'd kissed her last, though it had only been a day. She hadn't realized how hungry she was until his mouth offered her manna and she consumed it eagerly.

"You taste good," he murmured and kissed her again, exploring the warm sweetness of her tongue, then plunging to even deeper recesses. One arm circled her back, holding her snugly, the other hand rose through her hair to cup her head.

His embrace was masterful, sensually riveting. But Monica matched him with the caress of her lips and the play of her tongue, the slow stroking of her hands over his shoulders and back. She felt as though she'd been elevated, as though they'd both been elevated above their circumstances, above their differences, to a plateau on which they were man and woman at their finest. A heady illusion indeed.

Then came the knock, just as Michael had said it would. Unfortunately, though, he was only partly right. For the intruder barged through instantly, the end result being no different than if there had been no knock at all.

"Shaw? Hey—Shaw, what in the hell are you doing?"

Michael and Monica jerked apart, she with a gasp, he with a ragged sigh. Both pairs of eyes flew to the door. For Monica it was the moment of truth, the moment when her luck ran out.

"Well, well, well. What have we here?" The eyes of Fred Salazar were pinholed on Monica.

She stiffened. In response Michael's arms slackened their hold, but he refused to release her completely. "What is it, Salazar?"

But Salazar was still ogling Monica, whose stomach had begun to knot up. "If . . . it . . . isn't . . ." He drawled out each word, seemingly unable to believe she was there. But each passing second stretched his grin wider until it was thoroughly malevolent.

Monica stared at him in shock. Dark-haired and swarthy, he was in full uniform, as was Michael, yet he looked every bit as disheveled as Michael looked handsome. The contrast was appalling. Equally appalling to her was the fact that this man, the Public Information Officer of the Department, had been her nemesis, her major contact with the BPD for months. Now he'd found her in a compromising situation, and he was bound to make the most of it.

Michael, though, was still in the dark. Dropping his arms from Monica he turned to face his fellow officer. "What's this about?" he asked, his annoyance firmly leashed.

The villain looked from one to the other, Michael to Monica, then back. "You *don't* know, do you?" he asked, amused.

"Know what?"

"Who you've got here." Salazar's gaze raked Monica again.

When Michael looked at her as well, he caught a glimpse of the war between guilt, anger, and apprehension that was being waged across her features. He began to sense something was amiss. "What are you talking about?" he demanded, his question directed at Salazar while his eyes held Monica's.

"The Mouth. Right here in enemy territory."

"The Mouth?" Michael exclaimed, incredulous. It was a tag that Monica had known about for a while. Michael hadn't heard it before. "Salazar, what in the devil are you saying?"

"You've got her. Monica Winslow. High priestess of the airwaves. 'The Mouth,' as we affectionately call her." There was sarcasm mixed with venom in his tone. "The barbed tongue that regularly blasts Boston's finest for all it's worth."

Michael stood back, one hand on his hip. "Monica, what's he talking about?"

She held out a pacifying hand. "I can explain," she said softly, but Michael wasn't in the mood for softness.

"Is it true?" A muscle worked in his jaw.

"Oh, it's true, all right," Salazar broke in. "Her talk show has practically destroyed our PR department. But what's she doing here? Or is this a new approach, Monica? Seduce him, then stab him in the back?"

Had Monica not just emerged from a passionate interlude with Michael, she might have been more in control. At Salazar's words she winced visibly. Fortunately Michael came to the rescue.

"What do you want, Fred? Is there an emergency out there? I'm just about off duty."

Salazar gritted his teeth in an instinctive reaction to Michael's air of command. He knew that the issue of Monica Winslow would have to be dealt with later. "Your man. He hit again."

"The pickpocket? Where?"

"The Esplanade, not far from the Hatch Shell. You want to talk to the lady?"

"She's out there?" He tossed a glance toward the outer rooms.

"Pretty angry, but she's there."

Michael reached to massage his neck, then looked quickly at Monica before he spoke. "Okay, Fred. Hold her there. I'll be right out."

"What about *her?*" Salazar's gaze speared Monica again.

But Michael's vehemence deflected it. "She's *my* business. I'll take care of her. And if I were you I wouldn't broadcast the fact that she's been here, Fred. She's here at my request, very reluctantly, going through the mug book for me, looking for this same character."

"Is that what she was doing here," Salazar tossed out a final dig as his eye skimmed the room, "looking at mug shots—"

Michael stood straighter, clearly towering over the shorter man. "I said I would handle it."

"Okay, okay. I get the hint." The officer tipped his head in mocking deference to Monica. "*Miss* Winslow . . ." And he slithered back out, shutting the door behind him.

Four

His eyes betrayed little emotion as Michael quietly turned to her. "Monica *Winslow?*"

"It's my middle name," she explained softly. "I've always used it professionally."

He nodded, accepting the discrepancy. "Your program . . . ?"

"A talk show called *Speaking Out.*"

"Appropriate."

She shrugged. "It was meant to be."

"Was that your doing?"

"In part."

"But it's your program."

"I'm the host."

"Host*ess,*" he corrected her, seeming not

so much angry as curious. "You must be a
novelty in that respect."

"There are some others who have shows."

"But yours is the one that's caught on."

Monica smiled apologetically. "That's
what they tell me."

"How many hours?"

"Three. Eight to eleven."

"How long have you been doing it?"

"Four years. Since I came to Boston."

"You came especially for the show?"

"I suppose you could say that. I had a similar show in Phoenix, a smaller thing, one
hour a night. I'd wanted to come east for a
long time. When I sent out feelers to various
stations along the northeastern corridor,
WBKB picked me up."

"You must have come highly recom-
mended."

Again she shrugged, this time tucking a
lock of hair behind her ear. "I think it was a
case of good timing. BKB had just learned its
man was leaving, so there was a ready-made
opening. It helped that I had experience.
And the time I spent here talking with station execs didn't hurt."

"I'm sure," he drawled. Having had a
taste of her argumentative nature, he fully
understood how she could be a success in

her field. "How do you and Salazar come to be such, uh, good friends?"

"Isn't he a peach?" she retorted, her lips thinned in sarcasm. "Since he's the official spokesman for the department, he's the one I have to deal with either to try to get information or to justify the opinions expressed on the show."

"Yours."

"Yes."

"And you're really that rough on us?" There was something of an air of persecution in Michael's tone. She almost felt badly for him.

"You know my opinions."

"Oh, I certainly do. But to express them in private is one thing. On the radio, as the host of a show where thousands of people are hanging on your every word—that's another thing."

She actually felt guilty, and it annoyed her. "It's not that bad. Listening to Salazar, you'd think I devote a segment of my time every night to knocking the department."

"How often do you?"

"The department doesn't come up more than once every week or two and often it's in passing. People who call in are concerned about the quality of life in this city—naturally the performance of their police department is an issue. Believe me, there are many more fascinating topics for discussion than you guys."

"But when the issue of the police does come up, you're consistently against us?"

"I try to look at things reasonably but . . ." She looked at him askance, smirking sheepishly. "You of all people should know my feelings on the subject."

She wished he'd grin, then she'd know he didn't hold it against her. Looking at him, she was acutely aware of the dichotomy. There was Michael the man and Shaw the cop. Though she might hope for the respect of the latter, she desperately wanted the acceptance of the former. He didn't have to agree with her, simply admit her right to her own beliefs.

But he didn't smile. Not even a little. It was as though both man and cop suddenly had the weight of the opposition on his shoulders. They were indeed broad enough . . . but she wondered . . .

"Look," he finally muttered. "I've got to get into the squad room to talk with that woman." He darted a glance at his watch, then thrust his fingers through his hair. He looked tired.

"I thought you were just about off duty. Isn't the shift over at four?"

He gave her a pointed look. "The shift may be over, but the work continues. I'll have to speak to her now. If she's got something for us, I'd rather not let it go."

"That's dedication. I'm impressed." She'd said it in earnest, Michael took it as ridicule.

"Come off it, Monica! It's been a long day. The last thing I need now is your commentary. Save it for the show!"

As he glared down at her the sting of his anger worsened. Suddenly she'd had enough. "As a matter of fact I do have a show tonight. I was in the process of preparing for it when you interrupted me this afternoon. I really don't think I can spare any more time looking through your books." She took a quick breath. "And don't tell me about my responsibility. As far as I'm concerned, I've discharged it." She gasped again. "*And don't* offer to drive me home. I could use the fresh air."

Turning on her heel, she headed angrily for the door.

"Take a cab and bill us."

"I wouldn't want to be beholden to you."

"It's a long way."

"Not terribly."

"Hey!" His gruff tone halted her on the threshold, and she scowled back over her shoulder in time to see him mime a motion from the top of his head to the bridge of his nose. Grateful for the reminder, though furious that it had been necessary, she pulled the glasses from her head and put them on.

It was a token gesture at best. By this time Salazar was sure to have spread the word . . . unless Michael's warning temporarily postponed the inevitable. For it was inevitable. Word would seep through the department ranks like an ink stain on a blotter, dark and totally indelible. If only she'd been more cautious.

If only would do her no good now though. Trying to look confident and nonchalant enough to be adjudged a regular habitué of the police station, she moved from the private offices through the squad room, thanking her lucky star for her sense of direction as she retraced the route they had taken earlier. She kept her eyes lowered, feigning concentration, avoiding direct visual contact with everyone and everything. It wasn't until she'd actually covered several street blocks that she felt safe.

Safe . . . but frustrated, angry, and confused. So many emotions, so few explanations. Michael Shaw had a knack for turning her simple life topsy-turvy. What repercussions did she have to look forward to from this latest fiasco?

As she made her way through the business district in the straightest possible route toward Beacon Hill, her feet pounded the pavement with every bit of the vexation she felt. How *could* Michael have brought her there? How could he have gone ahead and *kissed* her? How could *Salazar* have barged in like that? Salazar, of *all* people!

Michael had seemed far more annoyed than embarrassed by the interruption. He certainly hadn't been intimidated by Salazar's having caught him playing on the job. But then, Michael hadn't seemed subordinate to anyone. Once more Monica wondered at his role in the department, this department in which methodical movement up through the ranks was the rule. Michael was an exception in many respects.

The walk home was not so long as tedious. It was a steady climb upward to the State House on the top of the hill, then a weary thudding, one foot after the other, down the even steeper incline of Mount Vernon Street. The afternoon was warm, rush hour had just about begun, and she still had work to do before the show tonight. A cab would have been faster, yet she needed the trek for its therapeutic value.

By the time she opened the door to her private sanctuary, Monica had exorcised the worst of her frustrations. What still lingered was an empty feeling, a feeling of disappointment that she wouldn't be seeing Michael again. There was no reason for any further contact, after all. He had assured himself that she'd suffered no aftereffects from her injury. He had returned her sunglasses and she his handkerchief. He had overseen her slow progress through pages of mug shots. As for anything else, she mused, it was destined not to be.

Headset settled firmly over her ears, she adjusted the volume controls and began. Her pleasant voice entered thousands of homes promptly at eight. "Good evening, and welcome to *Speaking Out*. This is Monica Winslow and my guest tonight is . . ."

It had to have been one of the driest segments she'd ever hosted. Monica felt herself stretched to the limit to ask intelligent questions of her guest. She'd crammed through the dinner hour at her apartment, studying the information she had so abruptly abandoned at Michael's arrival. It took her awhile to find her way again.

Never had she been more grateful for the support of her callers. Several were regulars and had the ability to spice up any conversation, regardless of how dull. There was Walter from Brighton, as the standard identification went, who railed against much of what the author had proposed as an indulgence of the well-to-do. There was Joshua from Hingham, who argued that tax sheltering was the privilege of the wealthy, since their money was adrenaline for the economy. And there was Paul from Bedford, who said that it was all a farce that the only way to minimize one's taxes was either to keep one's income near the poverty level or to emigrate. Paul was a true cynic, critical of most everything but guaranteed to draw a response from others. Tonight, in particular, Monica needed his help.

The B segment was far more exciting. Her guest was State Senator David Connelly, who had coauthored a bill establishing mandatory jail terms for drunk drivers. It was an emotional issue throughout the state, particularly well publicized following a series of tragic accidents in which a number of innocent people had been killed. The subject was all the more timely now, given the rush to pass the bill before the legislature adjourned for its summer recess.

At Monica's encouragement the senator expounded on his philosophy for a few minutes, explaining the history and content of the Connelly-Fox Amendment, as it was called. Monica interrupted only when she felt he'd said something that might be confusing to her listeners. In each case he patiently clarified the point. Then he offered his arguments in favor of the bill, emphasizing the deterrence value of such severe punishment as well as the obvious benefits of removing the offender from the streets immediately.

"But wouldn't a stiff fine and a license suspension accomplish the same thing?" she asked, launching into the counter-argument her listeners expected.

The senator was well versed in the debate. "License suspension is at best a diluted measure that has never proven to have any deterrence value. The same person who would drive while drunk would have no qualms about driving without his license. It's that I'll-never-get-caught mentality. We need something stronger. A mandatory jail term has that kind of potency."

Monica, too, was well versed. "I have to admit that Rhode Island recently instituted a policy of mandatory sentences from the second offense on. The police there claim that their citizens are terrified to get behind the wheel if they've been drinking. But what the police say and what proves to be true in the long run may be very different. And what about the illness, Senator? There are those of us who view alcoholism as an illness that can't be properly treated in prison."

David Connelly gave his opinion on that, repeating certain catchphrases, as politicians were prone to do. Monica questioned him on the statistics for drunk driving and on the trends of legislation nationwide. When she opened the line for calls, the keys lit up across the board instantly.

John from Revere thought it was unfair to use such a heavy hand to punish a first offense, that there should be a series of warnings, even more so than in Rhode Island, before imposing a prison term. When Monica asked if he'd ever driven a car while drunk, he hemmed and hawed, finally admitting that he'd been tipsy once. The senator asked him which would have kept him off the road most effectively—the risk of a simple slap on the wrist or that of a stint in jail.

He had no answer at all, and the point was made. Monica thanked him for the call and pushed the next button.

Chuck from Marlboro, her next caller, stated that alcoholism and drunk driving were far from synonymous. "A person who gets drunk for the first time may simply not know how to hold his liquor."

"That's a valid point," she conceded. "Senator?"

Connelly picked up on the argument instantly. "It's imperative for such a person to know beforehand that if he ever dares to drive, he'll be in trouble. There are alternatives after all—calling a cab or having a friend do the driving. That's precisely the kind of person who will be deterred by the threat of mandatory sentencing."

Monica frowned. "But precisely the kind who may be terrified *enough* by that first experience, particularly if he's stopped and given a stern warning, never to repeat the mistake. There's also the factor of court time and prison costs to be considered if we get into mandatory sentencing." She reached to answer another call.

"Hello, you're on the air."

"Monica?"

"Yes?"

"This is Nancy. I live in Quincy and my neighborhood is having an awful problem with teenagers. They may not be drunk, but they toss beer cans all over the place and race their cars up and down the neighborhood streets. It's a miracle we haven't had an accident yet. What can be done about these kids?"

"Not too much until they break a law," Monica replied.

"But what if they kill someone in the process? Half of these horrible cases you read about in the paper involve kids. Can we afford to wait until the damage is done?"

Monica yielded the floor to her guest, who expressed his utmost sympathy for the dilemma but could only agree with Monica that our system of justice did not allow for the possibility of preventive punishment. "All we can do if there is drinking involved with these kids is to let them know what might happen to them if they're caught."

"Of course they may be breaking other laws by disturbing the peace. A call to your local police might help. And in cases where there is a fatal accident, we get into vehicular homicide, a separate offense from drunk driving," Monica pointed out. "Let's hear from some of you others. Thanks for calling,

Nancy." She stabbed at another button to keep the ball rolling. "Hello, you're on the air. Hello?"

"Hi, Monica. This is Bill."

"How're you doing, Bill?"

"Not bad," the man said, with a hint of the shyness of one who was making a rare, if not his first call in to live radio.

Monica assisted him gently. "Did you have a question for Senator Connelly?"

"Actually," he began hesitantly, "I have a general comment."

"Uh-huh?"

"I don't see how mandatory sentencing can be considered fair when *all* driving offences seem to be policed so haphazardly." When he paused, she prodded him.

"Can you give us an illustration?"

"Sure. Speeding tickets. Ten cars may all be exceeding the speed limit, but the first in line will be picked up each time. The others zip on by while the first is being ticketed."

Monica grimaced. "Good point, but it's one you'll have to take up with the police. You're right. In that sense there is a certain random aspect to law enforcement."

When the Senator broke in to defend the consistent efforts of the police, Monica felt a spontaneous diversion in the offing. Sure enough, it happened with the next call.

"Hello, you're on the air."

"Monica? This is Louise. I want to agree with Bill about the inefficiency of the police. I live here in Boston, and it's gotten so that I think twice about walking anywhere carrying anything of value. The streets aren't safe. Forget muggers, the police can't even catch this dumb pickpocket!"

"*The* pickpocket?" Monica raised a brow. When had she asked *that* question last?

"Yes. It's been three months now, and he's still roaming the streets freely."

Monica paused to make sure her audience was following this. "For those of you who've missed it somewhere along the line, Louise is referring to the pickpocket who's been striking over and over again in some of Boston's finest neighborhoods. I understand he did his latest thing on the Esplanade this afternoon." She recalled all too clearly where she'd picked up that bit of information. "And as for your comment, Louise, you're right. The police do seem to be fumbling this one. It's frightening when this kind of thing can go on like this, time and time again." Senator Connelly and the Connelly-Fox Amendment were temporarily forgotten.

"Why can't the police do anything?" Louise asked in frustration.

"That's a good question. Perhaps some of you others out there may want to take a guess. The number here is 720-WBKB." The keyboard was already lit up. Nonetheless Monica wanted her audience to call in—or at least to try. "Give us a call and share your opinion on this or our earlier topic." She pressed another button. "Hello, you're on the air."

"Craig here, from Kenmore Square."

"Hi, Craig. Any insights?"

"Sure. I think the guy's doin' it for the fun of it."

"The fun of it?"

"Yes. He's pretty smart. Moves around without being seen. Probably dresses real well. You know, the kind you'd never think would be a crook."

"Just like you and me?"

"That's right."

"Okay. Thanks for the call, Craig." She punched the board again. "Hi, you're on the air. Hello?" A voice began to speak, but there was a telltale echo in Monica's ear. "Excuse me, but you'll have to turn down your radio," she reminded her caller, who promptly did so.

"Better?" he asked.

"That's fine. And you are . . . ?"

"Phil from East Boston. Why don't they double the patrols?"

Monica shot a questioning glance at the senator. "They claim they've got neither the money nor the manpower."

"With the hefty taxes I pay?"

"I know. It's really inexcusable. The money's going somewhere, but I'm not sure where."

"The guy hits only in certain areas. Can't they cover those places better?"

Beginning to feel like the devil's advocate, Monica found her own temper rising. "It would make sense. The fellow seems to specialize in Beacon Hill, the waterfront, and the Back Bay. He knows the streets like the back of his hand and always eludes the police without any trouble." She thought back to how he'd escaped Michael's partner. "Maybe he lives in one of these neighborhoods, though why someone who can afford to live there has to resort to thievery I don't know. Maybe Craig was right. Maybe he *is* doing it just for kicks."

"I'd bet that if the commissioner lived in one of those areas there'd be extra patrols," Phil noted.

At that moment, with all this talk of patrols, the image of Michael Shaw crossed her mind once again, and she felt particularly upset. Her eyes flashed an emerald green that no one but the now pensive David Connelly could see.

"Unfortunately," she began, driven by her own passion for the topic, "the commissioner is ensconced in his comfortable West Roxbury retreat. I don't think he leaves for his summer place on the Cape until after the fourth." Her voice dripped with sarcasm.

"He's up for retirement in two years, isn't he?"

"That's right. With a lovely pension coming."

"And then what about the department?"

Monica was well up on the functioning of the city government. "Then the mayor appoints a successor."

"Maybe *that'll* wake up the department," Phil commented.

But she was right on his heels. "Not if the new commissioner is another brother up from the ranks. Any speculation on who might be in line, Senator Connelly?"

The Senator came to attention. "I couldn't begin to speculate at this point. There are several qualified men in the department, and many more across the country if the mayor decides to look elsewhere."

"I guess we'll have to wait a while and

see." She sighed, moving on. "Thanks for calling, Phil. I think we've got time for one last call." A final button was depressed. "Hello, you're on the air." There was silence. "Hello?"

"What if I was to say that I'm your pick-pocket?" a flat male voice asked.

Crank calls were par for the course and even fun at times. This time, though, given the length and stress of her afternoon, Monica wasn't in the mood. It also occurred to her that she'd side-stepped the topic of the Connelly-Fox Amendment for too long. Finger poised, she quipped a calm "Then I'd say that you were pulling my leg" and cut him off with a final jab at the keyboard. "Those are all the calls we've got time for tonight. I'd like to spend a few final minutes with our guest. In case you've just tuned in, he's State Senator David Connelly, co-sponsor of the Connelly-Fox Amendment . . ."

Walking home in the dark across the lamplit paths of the Common, she thought back over the evening's discussion. Diversions often happened that way on her show, though the BPD was far from the only target. It was a spontaneous thing when it happened, a feeling shared by her callers and herself—though not necessarily by the segment's chagrined guest—that a breather from the original topic was in order. Often it related to an event in the day's news, as it had in the case of the pickpocket tonight, when callers' thoughts were running along similar lines.

For the first time, however, Monica felt somewhat guilty. That last call—she didn't usually turn one off like that. What if the man had actually been disturbed? Perhaps she should have tried to draw him out more.

Further she felt slightly fraudulent. Her own thoughts had been stimulated not so much by the department, the commissioner, or the pickpocket as by one Michael Shaw, whose image seemed to be imprinted on her mind. As valiantly as she fought it off, it was still with her. Was it presumptuous to wonder if he'd tuned in to the show? Mightn't he be curious, if nothing else, to hear "The Mouth" in action? "The Mouth," indeed. She wasn't *that* bad!

As she left the Common and started down Charles Street she thought of Michael and those penetrating eyes of his. Even now she had the eeriest feeling that she was being watched. She even spared a darting glance back over her shoulder before assuring herself that it was nonsense, just her imagination. With a defiant toss of her head she hurried home.

*   *   *

The next two weeks passed uneventfully for Monica, as though the incidents of that Tuesday and Wednesday had never happened. But the return of peace to her life was in its way both reassuring and frustrating, for those days *had* happened, and she couldn't totally forget the enigmatic appeal of Michael.

On that first weekend she drove out to the Berkshires to spend time with one of her sisters, who'd come east with her family to visit Tanglewood. It was a time filled with fun, a warm time for Monica to reacquaint herself with her nieces and nephew as well as with her sister and brother-in-law. And it was a time for them all to savor the rich strains of the Boston Symphony's Tanglewood contingent, a pleasure in any company.

Monday found her back into her routine however, busy yet naggingly empty. She poured extra time into preparations for the show, even made a point of lunching with friends several times during the week. Yet late at night, alone in her apartment, she returned to *Dreams of Ecstasy*, reading slowly, rereading favorite segments, pausing occasionally to daydream.

The second weekend arrived and with it two preset dates, one to attend a summer theater performance with a companionable

State Street stockbroker, the other to attend a Fourth of July celebration at the waterfront condominium of a psychiatrist, a man whom she'd met when he'd been a guest on her program and who had subsequently become both a good friend and advisor on matters relating to the show. It was Ben who had coached her on dealing with the toughest callers, and it would be Ben whom she'd consult if "the pickpocket" called again.

But he didn't. He struck five more times during the course of those two weeks, but she received no further call from a man purporting to be the pickpocket. The show proceeded smoothly with its usual mix of the light and the heavy, the sober and the humorous. Subconsciously at first, then more deliberately, she avoided topics relating to the police. It wasn't so much out of respect for Michael, since she assumed him to be a past acquaintance. Rather it was out of fear that she'd overreact—perhaps for that same reason. She couldn't seem to shake her sense of disappointment at the thought of never seeing him again. He had the makings of a hero . . . improbable perhaps, ill-fated perhaps, but a hero nonetheless.

On the Friday night after the holiday weekend, though, she could contain herself no longer. The pickpocket had struck for a sixth time since she'd seen Michael last, the sixth time being on that very afternoon. With so many other controversial matters on hold for the summer it was inevitable that her audience should pounce on the pickpocket. He was fast becoming a kind of cult figure with his hit-and-run style, never physically harming his victim, always leading the police a merry chase.

Her guest was the principal buyer for an exclusive Newbury Street clothing store and the topic, ingloriously enough, was unisex fashion. A woman had called to praise the wearing of male tailored suits with their bevy of inner pockets for wallets and credit cards and those flat but valuable things a pocketbook broadcasts to every thief around. It was a natural progression to talk of the pickpocket.

Jim from Billerica heckled her first. "He hit again today and you haven't said a word. You're not going soft on the police, are you?"

"I should hope not," she tried to make a joke of it. "You all know *my* opinion. Let me hear yours."

Jim proceeded to give his, a scathing denunciation of the BPD that even Monica felt to be slightly exaggerated. When she dared to suggest as much, several extra buttons on the keyboard lit up. The first and second split, one siding with Jim and one with Monica. It was the kind of sparring that she enjoyed from time to time. The third caller however took the fun out of it.

He didn't identify himself. That usually warned her. But she would never have dreamed to hear what he went on to say. "Rumor has it that you're personally involved with a member of the department. Could that be the reason you're backing off? Monica Winslow in love with a cop . . . now that would be something!"

At that moment Monica was eminently grateful that the medium of radio hid her face. For her cheeks had flushed a comely pink—almost incriminating in itself, even if the charge was false. She saw Sammy out of the corner of her eye, outside her soundproof booth asking with gestures if she wanted a cutoff. She waved him away and regained her composure.

"After a charge like that I believe you ought to give me your name," she began, her jaw clenched.

"The name's not important, but you haven't answered the charge" came the speedy rejoinder.

She was just as fast. "The charge falls flat, unless you'll identify yourself *and* the source of your information." She waited for several seconds. When there was no response, she addressed herself to the listening audience with a laugh of dismissal. "I guess that settles that. I'd like to thank all of you out there who *did* have the courage to identify themselves tonight. In the time that remains I'd like to ask my guest, Alex Thornton of J.M. East's, one last question . . ."

For the record she'd recovered beautifully. Privately, internally, the situation was less positive. It all came in on her during that dark walk home, myriad questions bombarding her from all sides through the silent loneliness of night. Who had he been? Why had he called? Where had he gotten his information? The charge itself was absurd! But Salazar had seen her in Michael Shaw's arms and must have spread *some* story. Who else knew? Where would it go from here?

Safely locked away in her apartment a short time later, she found herself wide awake as the questions continued to churn round and about in her mind. Feeling thoroughly unsettled, she undressed and tossed on a light robe, then sought solace as she often did in the summer night's calm of her balcony. This too had been a drawing card when she'd first seen the apartment. She spent much of her leisure time here, enjoying the fresh breeze as it rolled off the ocean,

across the harbor, and over the hill. Her
chaise longue was comfortably cushioned,
inviting her to sit quietly for a time.

But the mind was less docile than the
body. As had happened so often during the
past days when she'd caught sight of
Boston's finest, she thought now of Michael.

What if there *had* been something
between her and Michael? Certainly not
love, for they had far too many differences
between them. But what if they'd become
involved with each other in something beyond the stolen kiss along the line of duty?
How would that affect her work, her entire
outlook? He represented everything she'd
fought against for years, reason enough for
her to be grateful they'd seen the last of one
another. But, damn it, the man *was* attractive.

Seeking to rein in her emotions, she
reached for the book she'd tucked into her
pocket, switched on the small free-standing
lamp, and escaped into *Dreams of Ecstasy*.

She was lounging in the very same spot at
seven the next evening when the doorbell
rang. Frowning, she tried to imagine who
this Saturday-night visitor might be. She did
not have a date, had in fact planned to spend
a quiet evening at home.

Actually she was exhausted. She hadn't

gone to bed until nearly three in the morning, after she had finished the final page of her book. Then it had been a necessary struggle to drag herself up early enough to barbecue five pounds of chicken on the patio grill for the annual WBKB picnic at noon. It had been a fun gathering on the grassy banks of the Charles, a group of twenty of the people she liked and respected most. There had been good food, easy talk, a Frisbee or two, and much laughter. When she'd returned home at five, though, she welcomed the silence.

Now . . . the doorbell. Setting her white wine spritzer down on the low glass table, she padded over in her bare feet to answer it. "Yes?" she called through the intercom.

"You're home!" an exuberant male voice replied.

"Who is this?" But she felt a palpitation in her chest even before she heard his name. There was a richness in his tone that even the intercom couldn't suppress this time.

"Shaw." He paused. "Are you alone?"

"That depends. Is this war . . . or peace?" She hadn't seen him in more than two weeks, and they'd parted on less than affectionate terms. Then there was that bizarre incident on her show last night. Pray he hadn't heard . . .

"Peace. Are you alone?"

What the hell. "Yes."

"May I come up?"

"Uh . . ." She wasn't prepared for this, neither emotionally nor physically. But then Shaw always took her off guard. "Uh . . . sure," she finally answered grudgingly. "Come on up." Pressing the buzzer, she waited, leaning back against the wall, her head bowed. Last time she'd opened the door and followed his progress up the long flights of stairs. This time she simply closed her eyes to conjure up the image of the tall man dressed in blue bounding easily up the steps with a healthy spring of athletic grace. Her mind's eye saw that thick thatch of sandy-gray hair, the rugged tan, the chiseled features. What in the world was he doing here? she asked herself in alarm. If she'd been sensible, she would have kept him downstairs with some excuse or another. But it wasn't fun to be sensible all the time.

His bold knock quickened her already racing pulse. With a deep breath she raised her head, fluffed her mass of tumbling cinnamon hair with an upward stroke of her fingers, moistened her suddenly dry lips, and reached for the knob.

If only it *had* been Shaw the cop on the other side of the door. For the first time she realized what a natural buffer his uniform had been. Granted it had shown off his physique to perfection, making him look gorgeous and mysterious at once. But it had also been a reminder, tangible and hard to ignore, of his profession, hence his loyalties.

Now Monica was deprived of that buffer. Before her stood Michael, every bit the man, dressed in a sport shirt of a gentle pastel plaid, faded jeans that hugged his hips enticingly, and loafers casually worn without socks. On a whisper of excitement she caught in her breath. He was dazzling. Positively dazzling.

Five

Dazzling and breathtaking. Monica felt as though she'd received a body blow. It took her what seemed like an eternity of seconds to find a word, much less say it.

"Hi," she finally murmured, daring to smile in her own innocent way. It hadn't occurred to her that while she'd been taking in his startling appearance he'd done a bit of his own sightseeing. She'd never quite know whether the thickness in his voice was caused by excitement or exertion.

"I thought for a minute you were going to turn me away." Hands cocked on hips, he eyed her askance. "You really had second thoughts there, didn't you?"

"I wasn't expecting anyone."

"I'm glad. You look great." Passing up a second chance to rake over her slender form, his eyes held hers.

Only then did she realize what he must have already seen. She glanced helplessly down at her one-piece terry sunsuit. Elasticized at the waist and again just above her breasts, it was pure white and very bare, showing off the honeyed tan of her arms, legs, chest, and back in a way she wished was not so provocative. But it was cool, carefree, and comfortable, and she *had* planned to spend the evening alone.

"I'm sorry. Had I known you were coming I'd have dressed more . . . uh . . . more." She left it at that.

He quirked a brow in amusement. "Last time it was beer, this time a prim cover-up? You've got some weird notions, Monica Grant!" Those weird notions notwithstanding, she stepped back quite naturally to bid him enter, which he quite naturally did.

"I didn't mean that. Ach . . . maybe I did. But I was just out on the balcony relaxing with a drink."

"Sounds nice," he responded in a not-so-subtle way. But then he smiled, and any hesitancy she might have had vanished. It simply wasn't fair . . . what that smile did to her.

"Would you like one?" she asked softly.

"If it's no trouble."

With a shake of her head she gestured toward the patio. "Go on out and make yourself comfortable. I'll be with you in a minute. Is white wine all right?"

"Perfect."

She nodded her head but couldn't seem to move. It was as if his aura had overwhelmed her, holding her within its grasp. A willing victim, she indulged herself for a moment before mustering those last remnants of reason and forcing her traitorous body toward the kitchen.

Michael had taken her suggestion and was out on the balcony when she returned. With his back to her he was admiring the view of Beacon Hill climbing properly upward to the right and the Charles River sprawled far below to the left. The sun had begun to sink toward the river and now splashed its golden glow over water and piggy-backed buildings alike.

Transfixed, Monica admired her own view, the silhouette of Michael's statuesque frame enhancing the panorama she already knew so well. Then, lest she get carried away, she stepped forward onto the patio. "It's nice, isn't it?" she remarked quietly, letting her eye follow the direction of his.

"Beautiful." His voice was as quiet, even pensive. He turned and took the glass of wine she offered. "It's how I'd always pictured Boston to be—rich in culture on the one hand"—he looked up toward the right and the seats of business and government, then down toward the sail-dotted river—"pure relaxation on the other. It's very impressive."

His spontaneous choice of words triggered a memory that gave them both pause. In the instant they were back in the police station at the end of their last encounter. When Monica shifted her gaze, Michael's was there to meet it.

"I meant no offense." She softly spoke the words she'd ached to say since that day. "If it sounded sarcastic, I'm sorry. But I did intend it as a compliment."

She watched in fascination as his gaze melted to a liquid mocha. "I know," he told her. "I've thought about it a lot since. I . . . I guess I jumped to the wrong conclusion."

"It was the end of the day. You were tired." She made his excuse for him, but he refused to let it go as simply as that.

"More than that. I was annoyed that I had to learn the nature of your life's work from Salazar." With the way he spat out the name of the Public Information Officer, Monica felt they shared the same baleful opinion of the man. But Michael went on, commanding her attention. "Why couldn't you tell me yourself, Monica? Why the secret?"

She felt a twinge of guilt as she turned back to the serenity of the scene. "It wasn't ever really a secret. I just felt awkward." Her gaze fell to her hands, curled tightly around the wrought-iron railing. "I didn't want you to judge me as quickly and harshly as you would have if you had known from the start. I never really hid my beliefs from you—and they're the same, regardless of my choice of career."

"You're sure you just didn't want to be razzed in person? You know, it's one thing to dish out the criticism when your opponent isn't there to answer it. It's quite another when you chance being on the receiving end of that criticism. Looking back, I can understand the cause of much of your discomfort that afternoon—as well as your reluctance to come to the station right from the start."

Monica felt the reproof and jumped in to defend herself. "But that was only part of it! I meant what I said about having a visceral reaction to police-related *anything*. It's something I can't help."

"I know, Monica. I'm trying to understand that. But I still wish I'd known the *whole* truth. I might have been better able to handle things when Salazar broke in there . . ."

As his words trailed off her thoughts returned to that afternoon, that room, that kiss. Even now as she admired the masculine firmness of his lips she recalled their brand of warm persuasion. Even now she craved the same deepening sensation. But Salazar had broken in, and the kiss was ended. That had been it . . . until the call last night.

Her forehead puckered beneath her bangs as she thought of that spiteful call. Turning her back on Michael, she sank down onto her chaise longue, its back positioned for sitting and her knees bent up, and reached to sip her drink.

"I don't know who made the call."

"Wh-what?" Her head snapped up and she found him looking straight at her.

"Last night on your show. Salazar claims he didn't do it. But he did admit that it may have been any one of several others."

A gentle way of saying he'd talked. But Monica knew that. It wasn't Salazar's voice she'd heard last night. Of course he'd talked! She hadn't expected him to pass up such a fine opportunity.

"Didn't I say he was a peach?" she gritted, but Michael was more scathing.

"From what I've been able to see in the

short time I've been here the man does more harm than good. If it was up to me—"

"You'd boot him out? That's a laugh. Lesson number one about the BPD. Men simply aren't let go."

"Maybe things will change," he murmured half under his breath, but before she could challenge what she saw to be the improbability of his statement, he spoke more directly to her. "I'm sorry, Monica. If I'd imagined that would happen, I would have tried my best to prevent it. I know it must have caused a few difficult minutes for you. You handled it well." He stood facing her now with his back to the railing. The sun blazed low, hot, and orange, setting his features in higher relief, imbuing them with a more dramatic edge.

"I tried," she murmured, softly enough to hide the unsteadiness she felt. The heat of that evening sun seemed to intensify as it bounced from Michael into her. She took a sip of her drink, then concentrated on its dwindling supply of ice. "Did you hear much of the show?"

At the hint of movement she looked up to watch Michael lower his tall frame into the chair that was companion to her chaise longue. It was opposite her, respectably removed from her. "All of it."

"*All?* You really listened?" she asked, a pleased if puzzled smile on her face.

Michael stretched out his legs and casually crossed his ankles. Half-slouched but propped up on his elbows, he was the epitome of confidence. "Sure. Why is that so surprising?"

"Oh, I don't know." She shrugged and looked down again. "I just . . . didn't picture you as the type to spend hours beside a radio."

"Your show is good. I kept trying to turn it off."

Quite in spite of herself Monica smiled, then dared to face him again. "You did, did you? Fine friend you are!"

"That's a compliment. It was interesting. Actually it's been interesting each time I've listened. I really liked your interview last week with Dominic Anton."

So he *had* tuned in. Her eyes grew even brighter. "He's a brilliant director, and that was a simple show for me to do, since I adore the man's work. I've seen every one of his films, some more than once. Are you a fan of his?"

"Hmmm . . . sometimes." He made a vacillating gesture with one hand. "I liked his earlier films better than the more recent ones. But it's a treat to hear him talk."

"As articulate as they come . . . which is why I think he agreed to be on the show. When a celebrity—man or woman—has to rely on physical glamour to enhance his image, the medium of radio is the last thing he'll go for. A person like Anton, though, is fascinating just to listen to. Of course he knows it, and he can convert his appearance on the show into dollars at the box office. Not that I'm complaining from my end."

Michael studied her with those warm eyes of his. "You love your work, don't you?"

"Yes," she replied, buoyant with pleasure to be sitting in the sweet evening air with as handsome and companionable, and unexpected, a visitor as Michael. "I do love it. Each show is different, each one's a challenge. I get to meet interesting people, and then there's the discipline involved in reading their books—which may or may not be interesting." She snickered. "I've had to plow my way through a few."

"Like tax planning . . . or auto maintenance . . . ?"

That accounted for at least four nights that he'd listened. "You could tell?" she asked sheepishly.

Smiling, he broke it gently. "*I* could tell. Don't forget, I've seen you in person. Your voice has a certain ring to it when those green eyes of yours glitter. There wasn't any glitter when it came to the afterlife."

That was a fifth. "I'm flattered, Michael. You've listened to quite a few of my shows." Then she lowered her voice. "I wouldn't let your buddies know, if I were you."

"Are you kidding? I may not have known it until I started asking questions, but it seems that they all listen. You're the best and the cheapest form of entertainment around." Monica saw the mischief in his eyes and couldn't quite muster up the indignation. "They can throw their gibes at you from the sanctity of their homes, and you can't answer back. You're a dart board of the most therapeutic kind."

Surprised, she eyed him closely. "You have learned an awful lot in two weeks. As I recall you hadn't heard of 'The Mouth' when last we met."

"When last we met there were many things I didn't know. I'm learning fast."

"Oh?" she said, for lack of anything better. Why was it she could usually think so quickly on her feet? Finally she gave an exaggerated sigh. "Well, there's not an awful lot more you can learn about me. You're familiar with all the basic contradictions already."

When Michael leaned forward, she knew precisely why her usual quick thinking was now eluding her. He was so close, so virile, and she held her breath against the quiet force of him. "There are still all the delightful details," he shot back, his voice seductive even when he was teasing her. But he didn't so much as touch her.

"Not very interesting." She crinkled up her nose. It seemed critical to lighten up the conversation before she totally lost sight of it. "And, anyway, now that you know my profession and my particular gripe about men dressed in blue, I'd think you'd be wary."

"Wary? Me?" He shot her a punishing glance as he straightened up and sat back in his seat, allowing her to breathe for as long as it took him to finish the thought. "Certainly not! That's the challenge of it."

"Challenge? What *are* you talking about?" Before her bemused gaze, Michael stood and strode over to the railing. When he turned back, she saw a familiar determination etched into his features. "I've spent the past two weeks thinking," he began. "My first impulse when I learned who you were was to steer clear of you." He hesitated. "Then I realized that I couldn't do that." For an instant he looked like he was almost angry to have reached the conclusion he had.

"Why not?" she whispered. In an attempt at self-insulation she pulled her knees up and banded them with her arms. She couldn't have known how vulnerable she looked. But Michael knew.

His features softening, he stepped to the side of her chaise longue. The cushions pillowed her head when, entranced, she tipped it back. "Because we each have something the other needs," he stated with soft conviction. She started to shake her head, but he reinforced his will by sitting on the chaise by her hip and propping an arm against her far side, effectively imprisoning her. She felt the heat of his arm as it rested against her bent knees. Quite perversely her palms grew sweaty.

When he spoke again, he touched her soul. "I need a woman to share her life with me, to enrich my solitary existence, and stave off loneliness. And you . . ." He cast a glance at the side table, where, atop several magazines and another book, lay *Dreams of Ecstasy*. "You need a flesh-and-blood hero, a man to curb that tongue when it gets out of control, a man to give you another outlet for that passion."

He reached up and touched her face, sending shivers of fear through Monica. He saw far too much and understood that much more. She hated herself for it, but she was physically too attracted to him. Even now the tips of his fingers sketched her cheek and jaw in a way that shimmered warm awareness through cells that were utterly susceptible.

"No!" she gasped, on a stroke of resistance. "You're wrong."

"Am I?" His fingers now wove into the thickness of her hair, holding her head in place. "There must be something that appeals to you in those books or you wouldn't keep buying them. My guess is that the men in your life have always fallen far short of the kind of strength you crave."

"And you think you've got it?" she rejoined, gaining strength in the fight. She was partly lashing out against her own inability to deny his claim and in part against that very strength that drew her to him.

"I think so."

"An inflated ego. *That's* what you've got, Michael Shaw. Didn't I say from the start that it was an ego trip—police work? Here you are in a strange city for the summer, and already you've taken on both its insoluble problems, and me. What next? I thought you came here to learn—that was what you told me—to learn about the workings of a big-city department. Suddenly you're its conqueror." She gasped for air that seemed oddly thinner. "By the way I still haven't heard a word about this transfer program you're supposedly on. When did it start? And why hasn't there been any publicity on it?"

"Your eyes are glittering."

"You bet they are." She only wished she could move, but he'd penned her in. "And I'd like some answers. You're the most improbable policeman I've ever met. I still think you're an imposter."

"You ask too many questions."

She eyed him levelly. "No more than you did two weeks ago in that interrogation room of yours."

"It was my job."

"Well, it's mine too.

"You're not on the air now."

"That doesn't matter. Asking questions is part and parcel of my personality. Give me my answers, and I'll happily keep quiet."

"I can think of a much faster way to silence you."

"Spoken like a true male chauvinist." She sucked in her breath. "You're hurting my hair," she whispered, reaching back to try to relieve the pressure.

"Then hold still," he growled softly against her lips, and he kissed her with such tenderness that she couldn't have thought to move. Tasting the wine on his lips, she wondered if it were hers, but this was stronger and headier, undiluted by soda or ice. And it made her so dizzy that her mouth clung to his, helplessly. When he drew back she was speechless.

"A lovely state," he grinned. "Quiet and docile." He knew just which button to press for speech.

"I am not—" And which to switch to for silence. When he kissed her this time, there was a greater urgency, as though the first sampling had made him all the hungrier. His lips moved eagerly over hers, devouring resistance before it had a chance to arise.

As for Monica, she was too ready for his kiss to fight it without first savoring the reality of what she'd daydreamed of so often. Eyes closed, she opened to him, letting him explore her mouth with his tongue, then joining him in its intoxicating rhythm. This was the deepening she'd been denied before—this thrusting and sweeping, lips opened wide, breath mixing in heated gasps.

She trembled all over when she was finally released and laid back against the chaise, with her hips nudged over to make more room. Michael stared at her, his eyes ablaze with the same passion that rushed hotly through her veins. She'd known it would be like this. It was what she'd feared.

He had that power over her that no man had ever had.

Even now as his eyes lowered to her throat, then her chest, she wanted to cry out against him but couldn't. Rather she felt herself swell with desire, and she bit at her lip to stifle another kind of cry. Finally his gaze touched her breasts, caressing each in turn, with instant effect. The thin terry fabric of her sunsuit could no more disguise the hardening of her nipples than could its brevity present an obstacle to exploration.

With a beseechingly slow shake of her head Monica shrank back against the cushions. But his hands cupped her shoulders, lazily circling her smooth flesh before inching downward. "Don't, Michael," she choked, but he wouldn't stop.

"I won't hurt you."

"I know . . . but don't . . ."

He did. Following the route his eyes had taken moments earlier, his hands dallied just above the sunsuit's band before creeping down to touch her breasts for the first time. He explored their warm fullness in gentle rotating arcs while Monica moaned her agony.

"Michael . . ." She should hit him, jump out of reach, force him to stop . . . but she couldn't.

"Shhhh. I've wanted to touch you like this from the day I picked you up off the sidewalk. You're so soft and tempting." With the brace of his fingers splayed around her ribs, his thumbs brushed back and forth over her breasts' taut peaks. Monica felt a knot of fire growing deep within her, threatening to blind her to everything save the promise of bliss in Michael's arms. Unconsciously she squeezed her knees closer together.

"Please don't!" she gasped, but his lips covered hers to silence her once more. This time she grabbed his shoulders to restrain his advance, but even her fingers betrayed her, sinking into the hard muscle, drawing his body forward.

Unknowingly she had taken the first step. Michael swiftly took the second, lifting her into his full embrace. With his arm wrapped around her, crushing her to him, he buried his face in her hair and released his own groan of need.

For a fleeting instant Monica had no idea why she'd protested. It felt so good to be held like this by a man strong enough to take care of her. She rubbed her cheek against his shirt and pleasured in the solid feel of his chest beneath it. She loved the way he smelled and the way his body shielded her from the world beyond her balcony. To yield the reins of control for once and let pure passion take command—it was a luxury.

"Ah . . . Monica . . . sweet . . ." he murmured softly, his lips warm against her ear. He pressed her even closer as if trying to absorb her into his being. In response Monica's hands found their way across the muscled span of his back to lock behind his waist. Bizarre as it seemed, what Monica was feeling was almost like a sense of homecoming.

Through her contentment she became aware of a movement on her back, Michael's fingers gently exploring the warmth of her flesh, then slipping deftly beneath the band of her suit.

"No!" she cried, coming to her senses instantly. A hug and a kiss were hard enough to handle. Already she was aching with her own heightening need. But this . . . more and more . . . she didn't think she could bear it. "Don't!"

Holding her back only far enough to see her face, Michael framed it gently. "Why not?" he rasped. "It feels good, doesn't it?"

"Too good!" It was no time for false pride. "That's the trouble!"

"No trouble." His fingers traced the curve of her lips as though fascinated by their delicate lines. "If my touch pleases you, how can that be trouble?"

"You make me lose control," she protested, feeling it even now under the sensual heat of his gaze. "How can I think straight when you look at me like that?"

"You don't have to think straight. That's my job. You can close your eyes"—he did it for her with a kiss on each lid—"and let yourself go. Give yourself up to me. It'll be good for you." He planted a row of kisses across her cheekbone to her ear then ran his tongue around its sculpted shell.

"That's not . . . the point . . ." But she forgot what the point was when the back of his hand trailed down her neck to lightly brush her chest and she shivered in mindless delight. When his lips replaced his hand and his tongue began to trace lazy circles on the fabric just above her nipple, she let herself be lowered to the cushions.

But she needed more. It was as she'd anticipated—one taste of him was addictive. She needed his kiss now, full and firm. Boldly threading her fingers through the lush crop of his hair, she drew him up to her mouth, where she indulged her need, forgetful of all but the way he consumed her lustily.

In that moment he regained control, and

again things were new for Monica. For
Michael was simply not the type to put up
with the leadership in lovemaking of the liberated woman. He was the traditional hero,
the aggressor first and foremost, and it was
this very fact that excited her nearly as much
as that he was now touching her everywhere.

She moaned and sighed, returning his kiss
feverishly, lost to reason until she felt that
lightning touch of his man's rough hands on
the creamy-soft skin of her breast and knew
that he'd done it. Her sunsuit top had been
lowered to her waist, laying bare her full
feminine curves.

"No . . ." She tried to twist away in protest,
but his lips closed more firmly over hers, and
the words went unheeded in the cavern of
his mouth. He held her silent while his hands
cradled the gentle weight of her breasts and
his palms stroked their soft undersides.
When he began to manipulate her rigid nipple, rolling it back and forth, she couldn't restrain a cry. "Ah . . . Michael . . ."

"How's that?" he whispered against her
forehead.

"Good . . . oh . . . good . . ." she cried,
clutching his shoulders until her knuckles
were white, arching her back to offer more of
herself to him. Angling her hips in toward his
body, she felt as though she might explode.

"Michael . . ." she mustered a breathless plea when his touch grew even more intimate. She was in his care, being given what she wanted most at that minute. She thrilled to the feel of his fingers on her body, fingers that branded her *woman* and *cherished*.

Then he kissed her again and even more deeply, intoxicating her so wildly that it took her a minute to realize that his exploration of her thigh had culminated in a foray beneath her shorts, beneath the thin elastic of her panties.

"Oh, no . . ." she moaned, slowly realizing the extent of their indulgence. "You've got . . . to stop . . ." Breathless against his lips, she begged. "Please . . . ?"

Given another few minutes, they'd be in bed making full-fledged love to one another. Monica knew that, as surely as she knew that part of her wanted it more than anything. That part now was an agonized well of unfulfillment. The other part though was more sensible. To make love to Michael could never be a casual thing—it would be a commitment to pursue the relationship, and she didn't quite know if either of them could handle that. They appeared to be walking through life on different paths, crossing and criss-crossing occasionally, though each destined to continue his own direction.

That Michael had even heard her was a miracle. As Monica forced a painful return of self-control she realized the extent of his ardor, evident in the ragged chop of his breath and the strain of his muscles beneath her hands. But he did hear somehow, and he stopped, suspended.

"God, Monica . . . how can you ask that?"

"I've got to. I'm . . . not ready."

"You're ready . . ."

"That's not . . . what I mean."

"Then what, Monica?"

"I don't want this. Not now." Her breasts pressed against the fabric of his shirt until he set her back. Instinctively she crossed her arms to cover herself.

Michael too had begun to catch his breath. She watched as the smoldering light of his eyes flickered, then grew cool. "You're calling the shots?"

"On this? Yes."

"And that's how you like it, isn't it?"

"Not always."

"But with men you won't let go. Everything on your terms. Liberation and emasculation—they go hand in hand for you, don't they."

Stunned by his harshness, she simply stared. Then she quickly tugged up her top to cover herself again. "I couldn't emasculate you if I tried."

"But you sure as hell would try, wouldn't you?" he growled.

"That's *your* line, Michael. Don't use it on me! And don't make this out to be something more than it is." Sitting up straighter, she pulled farther away from him. "I thought you were different, that you had a sense of compassion."

"I do!"

"You do not!" She felt positively humiliated. "You're typical of your breed—angry that I won't satisfy your very basic need. Well, I'm saying that I'm not ready, and you'll just have to accept that. I won't be a handy receptacle for any man's lust!" Her anger was steadily building and wasn't eased in the least by Michael's even retort.

"I could have forced you, you know."

"Ahah!" she blazed away. "And now you're going to tell me that I'd have surrendered in the end, that it wouldn't have been by force at all." In a fit of fury she found the strength to scramble over both Michael and the arm of the chaise. Standing up to face him, she was trembling with rage. "You're right, you know. It wouldn't have been by force. I'd have given in and loved it." Her voice lowered to an impassioned whisper. "But I can tell you now that I would have hated you for it. Is that what you want?"

Whirling around, she fled from the balcony, pausing in the living room only for an instant's indecision. She couldn't stay in this room—he'd pass her on the way out. To fling herself on her bed would be melodramatic, to lock herself in the bathroom absolutely childish.

Her senses in turmoil, she collapsed at the kitchen table and threw her arms over her head as if to ward off the storm. But it continued to rage, and she didn't know how to protect herself. It seemed she was damned either way. By refusing to let Michael make love to her she should have been saved. Why then did she feel as though she'd behaved like a fool?

It was Michael. *He* did something to her, stirred her up until she wasn't herself anymore. Perhaps he was right. Perhaps it was a question of control. She'd never looked at it that way before. But then . . . she'd never been so very close to losing control before. It *was* Michael.

She sat at the table with her head down until she felt she had a hold on her emotions. No solutions . . . simply a hold. Then, with a long indrawn sigh, she sat up and cradled her chin in her hands. Was he still on the balcony, or had he left?

Then he moved. Monica jumped, her head jerking toward the door. So he'd been standing right there in the doorway, watching her all along. What had he seen with those penetrating eyes of his? And what did he want now?

The pounding in her chest began again as she waited for him to speak. But he studied her intently, seeing something in her face, considering something, debating something, finally chancing a crooked smile. Only then did his lips part for the deepest, the gentlest of voices.

"Do you like fried clams?"

Six

*F*ried clams? Monica stared at him in disbelief. "Fried clams?" How could he have vaulted so deftly from one appetite to another? For that matter, she asked herself, how could he stand there so utterly controlled? It simply wasn't fair! "Fried clams? Are you serious?"

"Completely," he responded quietly. "It's a nice night. We could take a walk down to the waterfront. I know this great place—"

Monica shook her head. "I don't think that would be wise."

"What? The clams, the walk, or the great place?" he teased, and she bristled perversely.

"None of it! The last time we risked getting caught, we were! And your man Salazar made sure someone heard about it. Can you imagine what might happen if we were seen together again? And after hours, no less?"

Michael assumed a carefree expression. "If the world already knows about our torrid love affair, what's the harm in a bucket of fried clams?"

Her voice was as miraculously level as her gaze. "There's no torrid love affair, and you know it!"

"Then why not take a walk with me? Seriously, Monica. It's nearly dark, and I can guarantee you that the place I have in mind is small and definitely off the beaten track for the average cop."

"As are you. Who *are* you? Really? And how would *you* know about this place if you've been in Boston such a short time?"

From his firm stance in the kitchen archway he undauntedly held her gaze. "If I promise you some answers . . . will you come?"

Catching the glint in his eye, Monica knew just what he was up to. Appealing to her curiosity, the rogue! But hadn't he already proven how well he could manipulate her by asking that one decisive question? And he always seemed to know the one!

"I still think it's a stupid idea." But she knew it wasn't the risk of being seen that bothered her most. Moments before she'd barely been able to break loose from his arms. Now to agree to spend more time with him and risk falling into them again? He was too potent, too virile, for comfort. And where he was concerned, she was all woman. Nonetheless, she *was* curious . . .

"Come on," he coaxed, cocking his head in such an innocent way that the harshness vanished from her face.

Sighing in capitulation, she relaxed. "I'm a fool is what I am for letting you do this to me. You must feel very proud of yourself."

She had expected him to enjoy the moment's opportunity for gloating, and she half looked forward to it, knowing that her time would come. But contrary to her expectations, Michael grew pensive. "Proud?" he asked, as if not comprehending. "No . . . not proud." When he frowned, he looked every bit of his thirty-eight years. "I'd simply like . . . your company."

Put that way, even despite the bait he'd already offered, she couldn't refuse him. Loneliness. That was what struck her. Indeed they had it in common.

Pushing herself from her chair, she spoke softly. "I'll be right with you." Disappearing into her room, she changed into her own pair of jeans and a fresh cotton shirt, which she knotted at the waist, slipped on a pair of navy espadrilles, brushed her hair, and brushed on a dab of pale pink blusher, then rejoined Michael.

As he had pointed out, it was nearly dark when they emerged from her building and started up the hill. There were other walkers along the route, some of whom Monica recognized as neighbors. But she felt comfortable. After his exchange of dress blues for denim and its more casual accoutrements, Michael looked no more like a member of the Boston Police Department . . . than she did. Looking up at him as they made the leisurely climb, she wondered again at his origins.

"Okay," she began with good-natured irony. "I'm listening."

"Listening?"

"Uh-huh. You bribed me by promising some answers. It's time to pay up."

But he just shook his head and looked mischievous. "Not until we've got dinner in front of us. If I tell you everything now, you're apt to turn and run back home. And I want the company for longer than that."

So did she, but she couldn't be quite as blunt. Despite her earlier arguments about the danger of being seen, she felt strangely at ease with him this way. In public there was less chance of the physical eruption that threatened to rob her of her sanity. It was dark, yes, and indeed romantic now, but all in a very gentle kind of way.

"How *do* you know about these little out-of-the-way places?" she asked.

His grin warmed her. "I eat out a lot. My own cooking is for the birds. Uh, better change that. Even the birds might get fussy when it comes to that."

"You can't be all that bad."

"Pretty bad. Oh, I can make things like toast, and I can pour myself a glass of juice. That takes care of breakfast."

"That's awful, Michael!" she exclaimed, knowing that the sturdy physique beside her needed far more nourishment than that. Yet she caught herself before she started to sound like a scolding mother, flipping from the role of protectress to that of the liberated woman appalled. "Do you mean to say that you never learned to cook for yourself?"

He shrugged. "I've never really had to."

"Spoiled from the start?" she taunted, but again Michael was unfazed. Nor was he smug. Simply blunt.

"I've been on my own for nearly twenty years now. I just hate to cook." He took her hand to pull her back from the curb while a car charged up one side of Joy Street and down the other. Her hand remained clasped in his when they slowly started across the street themselves.

"So you eat out."

"That's right."

"Doesn't it get tiring?"

He ventured a poignant glance in her direction. "Yes."

She nodded. What more could she say? Then she thought of something and blurted it out before she could think better of it. "You've never been married . . . or had a live-in someone?"

His chuckle was a rich, tickling thing. " 'Someone'. That's cute. Diplomatic."

Monica waited. She studied the handsome features of this tall man beside her and wondered how such a man could have spent a lifetime alone. "Well? Is it yea or nay . . . to either or both?"

He seemed to hesitate before taking the plunge. But he *had* promised. "Yea to the first. Nay to the second."

"You've been married?" she asked in surprise, then realized he'd only said he wasn't married now.

"Yes."

"You're divorced?" The obvious conclusion.

"Yes."

His terse tone made her think back to the vehemence of an earlier discussion. Then he'd lashed out at what he'd called the "libber type," and she'd gathered he must have been burned at some point. Had this previous marriage been that point? She wanted to ask but was stopped by the ripple of taut muscles in his jaw. Her answers could wait. It seemed more important to see his smile again.

"I'll have to do up my infamous Boston Baked Burgers for you some time."

It worked. A slow and skeptical smile crept across his lips. "Your *what?*"

"Boston Baked Burgers."

"That's what I thought you said. What the devil are Boston Baked Burgers?" As they passed beneath the State House arch, its light illuminated both their faces. For an instant they stopped.

Monica arched a brow. "If I told you, I'd be spilling the beans, wouldn't I?"

"I think you just did." He laughed. "But you're right. The surprise would be nice. And, besides, for every secret I pry out of you, it seems I have to offer something in return." He squeezed her hand and led her on. "I'll wait."

The golden dome of the State House was behind them now as they made their way down the opposite side of the hill toward City Hall Plaza and the marketplace beyond. Monica reflected on Michael's "offerings" and knew that only half of them were informational. The strength of his hand as it held hers so very gently attested to the world of other treasures embodied in this man.

They walked in silence for a while then, each enjoying the Saturday night life of the city with its summertime enchantment. They passed open air restaurants and brightly lit shops. They meandered among people similarly meandering, people of all ages, tourist and native alike. Amid the crowd they were anonymous, their faces dimly lit by the gaslights cordoning the walks of the harbor.

It was as though the shades of night had blunted their differences, as though they were a pair, a unit weaving among others. Michael guided her gently, his arm lightly around her back now to ease her beside him toward their destination. When they reached it, a small and private seafood house, Monica felt delightfully mellow.

"Did I come through for you?" Michael asked, bending down to murmur in her ear as he held her chair for her in true courtly fashion.

"You did." She smiled, giving credit where credit was due. "This is off the beaten track." Actually down several alleys and a harborside path. "I wonder how people find their way here."

"Not too many do," he replied as he settled into the seat opposite hers. "That's why it's so pleasant. Most visitors to the city would never hear of it. It mainly serves residents of the harbor area itself."

"And you?" she eyed him speculatively. "How did you find it?"

"I'm one of those residents."

"Of the harborfront? Really? Michael, these condominiums are all brand-new and phenomenally expensive. How did you ever manage one for the summer?" Perhaps it was rude of her to ask, but sheer impulse had gotten the better of her.

Undisturbed, Michael smiled smugly. "I've got connections. Friends in high places who could nail down a summer rental for me."

"Not bad."

"Not bad at all. It's a nice place and right in the heart of the city. I enjoy it."

"And you eat here often?"

"Maybe once a week or so. They've got a

lot of great stuff beside fried clams," he hinted, on a note of temptation. "Why don't you look at a menu and decide what you want."

Leaving the menu untouched in its place, Monica tilted her head sideways. "I've got a better idea. *You* order. Surprise me." It seemed like a fun idea and very different from her usual style.

"You're game?" His mouth twitched in the start of a daring smile.

"I'm game." She matched it.

Staring at her a moment longer, he seemed to weigh and balance the extent of her adventurousness. Then, without further word, he motioned to the waitress. Within minutes a bottle of wine had been uncorked and two glasses filled and raised in a toast.

Only then did Michael hesitate. Monica waited expectantly, wondering what sort of eloquence she'd hear. He seemed about to start more than once before catching his breath and beginning again. "Cheers . . ." he said at last, and she grimaced.

" 'Cheers'? That *is* profound."

"You've got something better?" he asked, amused.

"Sure," she replied boldly.

"Be my guest."

Monica looked toward the ceiling in

search of the right words. The ceiling was low and softly lit by candle-bearing sconces along the walls. But other than lovely patterns on a textured plane of white, the ceiling was bare.

Taking another breath she looked down at her hands. What could she say? To *us*? Certainly not. To the summer? Even worse. To the evening? Embarrassing. Her cheeks were faintly flushed when she finally looked up. "Cheers . . ." She echoed his toast with a sheepish grin. When he laughed aloud, the ice was broken. More elaborate toasts would be left for another time . . . perhaps.

Monica watched him sip his wine, watched its progress as it cooled his throat, watched as he set the glass down gently and captured her gaze.

"How is it that you're so well known around the city by name only? Salazar was the only one who recognized you that day at the station."

"Thank goodness."

"But why?"

"I purposely try to keep a low profile. There are certain things that I avoid—you know, newspaper or magazine interviews where they might want a picture, certainly television shows."

"Do you get calls often?"

"Not very. Local TV talk shows sometimes—but I refuse. I kind of like the
anonymity."

Michael pondered her words. "That's surprising. I would have thought that the visual
media would be the next step up for you."

"Not me." She shook her head decisively.
"I enjoy the job I have right now."

"No aspirations for the future?"

She shrugged, then frowned. "Some. Not
necessarily in the particular limelight you
mention."

"You'd be a great politician. You can talk
up a storm."

"Naw," she drawled. "A politician's life is
too hectic for me. I like excitement . . . and
then quiet. Like this." Again she surveyed
the intimate confines of the restaurant.
When her eyes came back to rest on
Michael, the sense of intimacy increased.
She cleared her throat in an attempt to keep
it within bounds. "What about you, Michael.
You're the one who's supposed to be on the
hot seat tonight. Tell me about yourself."

She admired the full arch of his brow as it
scattered furrows in its wake. "You know all
the relevant data."

"I do not! You're a thorough mystery to
me. I've told you before, but I say it again.
You're the most unlikely cop I've ever met."

"In what ways?"

She didn't have to think long. "Intelligence, for one. Or let me make that intellectuality. I get the feeling that you've had a lot more education than the average cop." When he simply dipped his head in silent admission of the possibility, she probed deeper. "Tell me what degrees you hold."

He moved his wineglass to make room for the salad that chose that moment to appear at their places. Monica studied the creation before her and nodded her approval. "This is quite a salad. There must be three kinds of lettuce here, not to mention zucchini and chick peas and bean sprouts and alfalfa sprouts." With the help of a fork she peered beneath a carrot curl. "Artichoke hearts? I love them!"

Michael popped a cherry tomato into his mouth and smiled at her pleasure. "You've forgotten to mention cucumber and tomato and Spanish onion."

"Oh, those are ordinary. But this other stuff . . . good show, Shaw!"

His smile held his satisfaction. "Not mine . . . but I'll take the credit if you insist." Then he paused. "Tell me about your childhood, Monica. Aside from the, uh, police incident, I know nothing."

"Oh, no," she came back as she nonchalantly sucked the pit of an oversized black olive. "You aren't getting off that quickly. Where did you go to school?"

"The West Coast."

"Where?"

"Stanford."

"Undergraduate?"

"That's right. I did my graduate work at Cornell."

Tilting her chin up, Monica put down her fork and faced him pointedly. "If I were to use my imagination based on what I've seen of you, I'd bet you have a law degree." When he grinned, she grew buoyant. "Am I right? You do?"

"Yup." As implausible as it seemed for a policeman, it fit Michael to a tee.

"Did you ever practice?"

"Some," he answered more evasively, then led her on a different tack. "There was actually a stint in the army in the middle there. The GI Bill pretty much put me through law school."

The outermost edges of the mystery were finally beginning to sort themselves out. Monica felt a mild sense of triumph that her instincts hadn't failed her. She'd known he was different. "Aren't you overqualified to walk the beat?"

"I don't always walk the beat. There's plenty of desk work to do—"

"You know what I mean. Isn't there some way to use your legal background in your work?"

"I do. Every day. It gives me a far greater insight into what is and what is not effective police work."

"I'm . . . not sure I understand."

Michael spoke gently, patiently, yet she could hear the same sense of determination she'd heard before when he'd talked about his work in the most general terms. "You know as well as I do that the police across the nation have come in for criticism over the years in large part because of arrests that never stand up in court for one reason or another." She nodded and he went on. "There's no point in apprehending a suspect if the evidence is either insufficient or so ineptly gathered that the case will fall through. I can be careful in what I do. I can try to see that others are as careful. You may call the average cop an egotist, but I honestly believe that much of it is just overzealousness." For the first time she heard a note of accusation and knew it was directed at her.

"It may well be," she argued, "but how do you control it? You're the exception—"

"That's where you're wrong. I'm no exception, Monica. Do you know how many men are getting advanced degrees? Oh, maybe not in rural departments or in certain areas of the country. But in the larger cities like this one—the percentage rises every year."

She snorted, and briefly reverted to type. "You could've fooled me!" But the spark in Michael's eye held further sarcasm in check.

"Change takes time, Monica. And it takes an open mind to recognize it when it happens. I've met some pretty dedicated men in the department since I arrived here last month."

"Like Salazar?" She couldn't resist the jab but regretted it quickly.

"Salazar is the other extreme. You already know my opinion of him. He'll have *his* day of reckoning."

"You sound so sure," she remarked skeptically.

Michael diverted his attention to his salad, ate for several moments, gathered his thoughts, then spoke with quiet conviction. "He'll get his. Take my word for it." His expression was nearly as grim as his words.

"Now *that* sounds like a personal threat. Has he made things difficult for you?"

"Not really. But I've seen him operate around the department, and, frankly, he's offensive. For a man whose job it is to improve relations between the department and the community, he's blown it."

Monica's sigh preceded a soft-spoken "At least we agree on that."

Two hours later, as they slowly retraced their steps from the waterfront through Government Center, up over the hill and down again to her place, they were still in agreement. The meal they'd shared had been delicious, every last shrimp, scallop, and oyster that Michael had ordered.

"I feel absolutely stuffed." Monica let out a forced breath. "I only wish I had the strength to jog up and down the hill a few times."

"Do you jog?" he asked, gazing down at her as they walked.

She shook her head. "I ski in the winter and swim in the summer, but more often than not I walk. Anywhere and everywhere."

"So I haven't tired you out tonight?" There was that tiny twinkle in his eye, barely visible in the light of the streetlamp as they passed, that hinted at mischief with a very definite, if subtle sexual undertone. It suddenly occurred to her that he'd been a perfect gentleman all evening, relating to her as a total person as opposed to a strictly female one. Of course, there had been that balcony scene earlier . . .

She shook off the thought determinedly. "Certainly not! But . . . what about you. What do you do for exercise?"

"I run."

"Long distance?"

"That's right."

"Then you're in the perfect place," she exclaimed. "You have no idea what happens here in the spring. People come from all over the world to run in the Boston Marathon." Her breath caught at the next thought. "But . . . that's not until next April. You'll be long gone by then . . ."

The question wafted off into the evening air as they both reverted to silence. He would be gone. Was she sorry? A surreptitious glance told Monica that he was embroiled with some deep thoughts of his own. His brow was creased, his jaw set. Then, as they rounded the corner onto West Cedar, he emerged from his abstraction.

"You once said something about having a car. Do you still?"

She recalled the reference. It had been that Wednesday afternoon, over two weeks ago, when he'd railroaded her into going to the police station. "I did when I first came here, but I found I didn't need it, living on the Hill. When I can't walk, I use the T. On those occasions when I want to drive somewhere—for the weekend or whatever—I rent a car. It's much easier and cheaper in the long run. You know, insurance and parking. With the way you guys ticket cars around here, I'd be in grand trouble."

She thought he'd react in some way to her tongue-in-cheek barb, but he didn't. He was hung up on another thought. "Does the station reimburse you for cabs?"

"Cabs?" She shrugged. "I rarely take them."

Michael stopped still before her building. "Then how *do* you get home from the station in the middle of the night?"

"It's not the 'middle of the night.' It's only around eleven thirty or so. And I walk," she stated, having likewise halted to look up at him. The look of displeasure she saw was raw and angry.

"You walk across the Common alone, late at night?"

"It's a quick walk."

"That's insane, Monica! It's dark and deserted—"

"It's not! There are lights and people. And, of course, you fellows have your regular patrols." Her scorn was muted, but not to be missed. Michael didn't.

"You know as well as I do that we can't be everywhere at every minute. How long do you think it would take some bruiser to clamp a hand over your mouth and drag you off into the bushes?"

Monica lowered her head to grope in her purse for her keys. "You're being melodramatic."

"I'm being realistic!" he boomed back. "You seemed to feel that's *your* specialty, but I can tell you, lady, it isn't!"

"Quiet, Michael," she warned as she unlocked the door. "You're making a scene. I wouldn't want to have to call the police," she said mockingly.

The door was pushed open, and she was ushered straight into the lobby. The hand on her elbow didn't yield, but his voice was lower. No less harsh . . . just lower. "Don't be smart, Monica. One of these days that mouth of yours may get you into real trouble."

"Let go of my arm," she demanded, but he simply kept pace with her as they reached the stairs, rounding the first flight, then the second, until they were standing before her door. Before she could think, Michael had removed the keys from her fingers, unlocked the door, and propelled her through the doorway. When he shut the door and leaned back against it, she sensed the oncoming storm. There was an anger in him now that she couldn't comprehend.

"What *is* the matter?" she asked, trying her best to face him calmly. "It's no big thing—my walking home at night."

"Perhaps not to you," he growled. "You haven't seen the women I have. Women who've been beaten and raped and robbed and permanently scarred, psychologically if not physically."

"Boston isn't a jungle—"

"It's no paradise either! Don't delude yourself into thinking it can happen to anyone else but you. You're taking a terrible risk!"

She faced him defiantly now. "It's my life. I've done fine for twenty-nine years."

"Have you?" he retorted just as strongly. "Have you really? Is that why you were as lonely as I was before I got here tonight? You were glad to see me . . . and don't try to deny it."

"I won't." She tipped up her chin. "I did think the company might be pleasant. And it was . . . for a while . . ."

"But now you'd rather go back to your books. Is that it?" he speared her mercilessly.

For a moment Monica could think of nothing to say. "You don't pull any punches, do you?" she murmured at last.

"I say what I see. And what I see is a woman in limbo."

"You're wrong. I know exactly where I am and what I want."

"You do? Is that why you stay home alone reading? Is that why you come alive in my arms and then back off as though you were a virgin? Is that why you've got that carving of a mother nursing her child on your mantel?"

Glancing back at the carving, she felt a twinge inside. But her own anger had been piqued, and she turned to Michael with flashing eyes. "Of all the arrogant . . . Who are *you* to analyze me? Just because I let you take me to dinner doesn't mean I need your lofty diagnosis. Limbo? I'm very pleased with my life in the here and now."

"But what about tomorrow? Do you really know what you want? For a feminist, your behavior's been purely feminine tonight— from that bit on your balcony on. You let me order . . . you didn't insist on separate checks the way a true feminist would have. No, Monica, you let the mask slip tonight. Very comfortably. And much as you might argue to the contrary, you need something more from life. Not all women do. But you— you need a man."

Trembling with fury at his assault, Monica gritted her teeth. "I don't need you. I think you'd better leave."

Michael lowered his head, then raised it

just a bit to look at her through spiky brown lashes. Slowly and with devastating implication, he shook his head.

"What do you mean—no?" she asked, her voice a tone higher.

"I'm not leaving yet."

For the first time she was actually frightened. There was that determination in his eye. "What do you want, Michael?" she asked, wondering if there was an entirely different side of the man she still hadn't seen or imagined.

"I want you. You know that."

"I'm not for sale. Not for a dinner . . . or information . . . or anything else you have to offer."

"No?" he asked with such pointedness that her stomach knotted.

"No! And I know karate. If you come near me"— she began to back away from him— "I'll hurt you."

He took a step forward. "I think I can protect myself. I'm bigger and stronger than you are." He took another step.

"Michael, why are you doing this? It's crazy! Women aren't supposed to be forced!" Her mind was a flurry of activity. Her alternatives—what were they? Somehow she couldn't think straight. As he advanced she retreated. She was near the kitchen . . . or the bedroom. Only the bedroom had a door. No lock though. Could she hold out against him? And the only phone was in the kitchen. How could she call for help? Help? He *was* help.

As though he were reading her mind, Michael grinned. "Feeling cornered? Isn't that how your heroines feel when their swarthy hero has them trussed up and on the verge of surrender?"

"I think it's *you* who read these books. You seem to know an awful lot about them. Maybe it's your life that has something lacking?"

The mistake had been made and couldn't be erased. Monica knew it even before he moved quickly to snare her in his arms. But she fought. With every bit of her strength she pushed against his chest. He simply tightened the bonds, imprisoning her with one arm around her back and the other hand in her hair. When he tipped her head back, she had no choice but to look up at him.

"Perhaps you'd like to repeat that sweet thought," he rasped.

"Let me go."

Again he shook his head. "There's a point to be proven here, and I have every intention of proving it."

"Michael, please . . . let me go."

His lips lowered to stifle all sound then, punishing hers with the force of his anger. She held her mouth rigid and tried to twist her head away, but he only tugged harder on her hair. When she cried out, she unwittingly gave him the opening he sought, and he plundered it instantly, ravishing the inside of her mouth as she strained against his arms. But she was held tight. Only her legs were free and with these she launched her counterattack, kicking at his shins, trying to forge enough of an opening to bring a knee back and up. One good shot. That was all it would take . . .

Her design must have been transparent. For within an instant Michael had torn his mouth from hers and hoisted her off her feet completely and into the prison of his arms. Denied the hope of disabling him, she struggled frantically. He was bigger and stronger—as he'd said, as she'd known. By the time he dropped her on her bed and hovered over her, the best of her energy was drained.

"Michael!" she gasped. "You're mad!"

He pinned her wrists above her head and immobilized her with the solid strength of his body. "Mad?" he asked, more gently now. "Not mad, Monica." She could see the hard line of his jaw by the light that poured in from the hall. "Crazy. Crazy to be attracted to trouble. That's what you are—trouble from the word go. But damn it if I don't want you all the same!"

He could easily have taken the line out of any of the books on Monica's shelf. Eyes round with confusion, she stared up at him. He was the prototype of a hero, tall, lean, strong, and with a will to match. The faint tremor in his arms as they pinned hers to the bed, the tightening of his muscles as they bore into her more pliant flesh—oh, he did want her. There was no doubt about it. But who was *she*—that traditional heroine . . . or Monica? Suddenly she wasn't quite sure which she wanted to be at this particular moment. But either way she'd fight him.

It took one firm contortion of her body, a futile attempt to displace him, for his lips to swoop down and seize hers again. "No!" she cried when he allowed her to draw a breath, but his body had clamped itself so throughly against hers that she could neither kick nor hit nor even twist beneath him. "Please . . . you're hurting me . . ."

But he continued to kiss her, conquering her mouth with a sally that robbed her of breath, leaving her nothing but soft moans of dying resistance. For the onslaught was now coming from two fronts. There was Michael, whose mouth seemed suddenly virile velvet over hers—and there was herself. Her body. Aware of every hard contour of his. Curious. Straining. But toward or away from . . . therein was the conflict.

"Why do you fight me, Monica?" he moaned against her neck, where his lips sampled the honeyed warmth of her skin as she rolled her head to the side.

"You have no right . . ." she gasped, fighting her own body as well.

"I want you." His breath fanned the hollow of her throat, moving downward. "I *need* you. That's my right . . ."

When she felt his lips on that low vee of her blouse, she wrenched the few inches she was able to. He raised himself then, clutched both her hands into one of his and captured her chin with the other.

"Ease up, Monica," he commanded with a growl. "Or is it the fight you need to preserve your virtue?"

"You're wrong! I have a right . . . to a choice," she panted, struggling now to free her hands but quickly learning of the power of his one huge fist. "I don't . . . want . . . you . . ."

"No?" he seethed as though he, too, were fighting an unseen foe. "We'll see about that!" And he kissed her again while he held her head still. But this kiss was different. Miraculously so, through his anger . . . but it was gentle and persuasive in the same way he'd kissed her at other times. If he'd been hard and forceful, she might have been able to maintain her will to resist. This heady sweetness though was something else.

"Stop . . . !" she begged, but he plunged further, his tongue occupying the far recesses of her mouth, moving against hers with catlike seduction, riveting her senses to the exclusion of all else. She hadn't even realized he'd released her chin until the last button of her shirt was freed and the material spread wide.

He had levered himself onto his side, with one leg still holding hers in place. With a deft motion he brought her wrists down to shoulder height and lowered his head. When his lips touched the first swell of her breasts, she gasped. "You can't do this to me . . . Michael . . . !"

His mouth moved against the rising fullness. "I can . . . and I will," he murmured, slowly inching his way toward that sensitive tip. When he reached it, she cried out, but now in the agony of desire as his lips opened and took her in. Red-hot charges shimmered through her, fed by the tongue that rolled her nipple to a peak and the teeth that drew the essence from her.

"Michael . . . please . . ." How many times had she read it? Did she want him to stop or go on? She *didn't* know!

At least having the grace not to ask, Michael moved up on her body again, releasing her hands in a tentative gesture. When she made no effort to fight but simply stared at him in bafflement, he slowly pushed himself up to straddle her legs. She was aware of feeling more frail, totally vulnerable beneath him, was aware of the heat of her desire so close to his. She couldn't say a word when he began to unbutton his shirt, could only hold his gaze as he held hers.

Then the shirt was gone, and she couldn't resist. Fearful of her own reaction, she looked helplessly at his chest. It was broad and powerful, lean but muscular. She wanted to touch him and curled her fingers into a fist to prevent that self-indulgence. There was still a battle of wills between them, and she refused to give him the satisfaction of knowing how handsome she found him.

He had no such qualms, however. Spreading her shirt further to the sides, he admired her openly. "You're beautiful, Monica," he said hoarsely. "Very beautiful." His hands traced wide circles around her breasts, and she clenched her jaw against the havoc they wreaked. Closing her eyes, she tried to think of anything but the exquisite intimacy of his touch. It was useless. Moaning softly, she squeezed her eyes tight, then put her hands in motion to grab at his wrists. But he reversed this motion instantly, and her eyes flew open in time to see him pin her hands back to the spread and lower himself over her.

Their flesh met and sizzled. Monica felt as though his strength was her reward, and she'd never been as happily rewarded before. He moved slowly on her, heightening the friction of her breasts against the soft-haired texture of his chest. When he found her lips once more, it was more fiercely. Even this fierceness was different though. Before he'd been angry, now he was a man aroused and hungry. Monica was no less so.

When he released her hands, she touched his back, smoothing her palms upward along the sinewed cords, pleasuring when each muscle responded to her with a flex and a quiver. So there was power in this power-lessness, she mused, mindless at the moment of her imminent surrender. His hands re-turned each caress, stroking her with awesome effect until she had no will to fight. She needed Michael. Fully. The emptiness inside ached for him.

Writhing against him, she held him tighter. He kissed her again and again, devouring her moans of pleasure and answering her straining body with his own. Suddenly Monica didn't care who she was. She could as well have been that fictional heroine finding passion's glory in her hero. "Michael," she moaned, wanting him now. "Michael . . ."

His hands made short work of the snap to her jeans, and he angled himself away from her enough to tug at the zipper. When his fingers slid down against her flesh, she arched her body instinctively. Her breath came in shorter gasps as reality slipped slowly away. This was her hero above her, making her body feel so divine. But there was nothing timid about this heroine. She needed him closer, deeper. She needed to touch him as well.

Between intermittent sighs and moans that punctuated the soft night's silence Monica rose to meet his kiss with an ardor that startled them both. Her fingers followed, wandering the warm expanse of his chest with reckless abandon, touching those twin spots she knew would excite him.

"Ahhhh . . . Monica . . . that's it . . . ahh-hhh . . ."

Excite him she did, even as she excited herself. Bending one knee up to allow him more freedom, she thrilled to his deeper exploration. His fingers stroked her with precision, knowing just where and when and how.

In a burst of passion she reached to touch him as intimately. When her hand cupped his denim-sheathed thickness, he rasped her name again. But it was the rest of his body that stiffened as well when she began the gently caressing motion intended to render him as helpless as she was.

Michael was not about to be rendered helpless. As though shocked into instant awareness, he withdrew his hand and clutched at hers to still it. "What is it *you* want, Monica?" he asked. The choked sound of his voice was small solace for its unexpected chill.

"You, Michael," she gasped. "You!"

He took her hand and pinned it to the spread until he was looming over her. His eyes still smoldered with the passion she knew stirred within him, but his features were suddenly taut. "You want me to make love to you?"

"Yes," she whispered, stripped of all pride in the wake of his sensual victory.

"Right now?" His chest rose and fell above her.

She offered a breathless "Yes."

"Why?"

Why? How could she think? "Because . . . I . . ."

"Why, Monica?"

This wasn't how it was supposed to happen, she protested silently. He was supposed to take her—no questions asked! What kind of hero was he? Perhaps not as much in the traditional mold as she'd thought? Perhaps he *was* concerned with what she felt? Or was it all part of the torment, the humiliation?

"I need you, Michael," she whispered, knowing the pain of emptiness more acutely than ever. But when she needed his embrace above all, he pushed himself up and off the bed. Standing with his back to her, he hung his head and worked at the muscles of his neck.

Stunned, Monica clutched at her shirt, pulling it closed and inching up against the headboard of her bed. Her voice trembled audibly. "What is it? What's wrong?" She'd never been rejected this way before. Nor, for that matter, had she ever pleaded for a man to possess her. It was a new chapter in her own book, and she felt bewildered.

"It won't work," he announced darkly, his shoulders bent now in an attitude of fatigue.

She stared incomprehendingly. "*What* won't work? You were as aroused as I was . . ."

Very slowly Michael turned, then as slowly he forced a lopsided smile. "That was supposed to be my line, wasn't it?"

"It doesn't matter!" she exclaimed. "I just don't understand!"

"Then let me spell it out," he growled, the smile a faint memory, now replaced by a scowl. "T-R-O-U-B-L-E." Leaning over with his fists propped on the bed, he raged quietly. "I've never forced a woman in my life! Yet I nearly did . . . because of you!" He rose to his full height, raked a hand through his hair and stalked toward the window. "My God, I'm a fool!" This time there was self-hatred in his voice, and Monica had to know the reason.

"Why? Tell me, Michael."

The silence was deafening. She felt the heavy beat of her heart and wondered that its vibration didn't echo in the night. Reaching over to one side, she flipped on the lamp. Michael's back was broad and tanned, glowing beneath the barest sheen of perspiration. With his hands cocked on his lean hips, he seemed to be waiting for something, some command or direction. Lowering his head, he shook it slowly, then turned toward her. His eyes were full of sadness, his words full of regret. Only his voice betrayed anger.

"My wife was like you, Monica. I guess I'm attracted to the type. Intelligent. Witty. Challenging. Individual. I spent the three years of our pathetic marriage trying to keep up with her brilliant ideas. She was the modern woman, through and through. Enterprising. An activist. It took me all that time to discover that while she may have been great in bed there was no lasting warmth to her. Perhaps she was incapable of deep love . . . I really don't know."

"You shouldn't be telling me all this—"

"Why not? You wanted to know what was wrong, and I'm obliging you," he shouted before lowering his voice and leaving the boiling rage for his eyes to express. "What's *wrong* is that I want a woman—a *real* woman. I want a woman who knows when to do her thing and when to ease off. I want a woman who *needs* me as well . . . because I'll sure as hell need her! And I *don't* want to have to arouse her to a frenzied state before she can make up her mind! *My* woman is going to sit out there"—he made a random gesture toward the city beyond the window—"and want me, even when she's far away from me and embroiled in her own world." He paused, breathing heavily, his nostrils flaring with the exertion. Then he moaned and swore beneath his breath. "Damn!" And as Monica looked on disconcertedly, he hooked a hand beneath the shirt he'd let fall to the bed and vanished without sparing her another glance.

It wasn't until the wee hours of the morning that Monica was able to accept what had happened. She had indeed been rejected, and for good reason if Michael's tale was true. He wanted total commitment from a liberated woman. Was that possible? *Could* a woman be liberated while being fully committed to a man? Or were the two states incompatible? She'd begun to wonder about similar things of late herself . . . and she simply didn't know the answer. She knew that she loved her work and she loved her freedom. Then there were her books and the penchant for romance she'd developed. Was Michael right in his analysis? Was she in a kind of limbo, dangling between the woman she was at times and the woman she yearned to be at other times? Was there no happy compromise?

She anguished late and woke up early, determined to pore through the Sunday paper from the front page to the want ads. Yet her mind wandered to thoughts of Michael. He would have been here now . . . had he stayed. She might have cooked him breakfast—a real breakfast, fit for the man he was—and they might have shared the paper. Alone it seemed far less appealing.

Aimless steps took her out onto the balcony. The warm breeze ruffled the gauze of her robe as she stood at the railing, admiring the city before her. Where was *he* in all this? she asked herself. Was he spending the day alone too?

With a sigh of resignation, she settled onto the chaise. This was no day for the Sunday paper. What she wanted was *Passion's Challenge*. Without a care for the why of it all, she reached for her book and opened to Chapter One. She was right back at the start.

The fact had never been as clearly driven home as it was that very evening. Dressed formally in a simple white silk gown that shimmered from ankle to shoulder, with its share of scoops and slashes along the way, Monica attended a dinner reception given by the mayor to honor the visiting conference of his fellow New England mayors. She was but one of many media representatives invited. Indeed she arrived on the arm of the news director of one of the local television stations, similarly formal in his white-topped tuxedo, and good-looking to boot. They made a handsome pair, moving quietly from group to group as a bevy of hors d'oeuvres made the rounds. It was only when dinner was about to be served that she looked up, laughing at an amusing anecdote, to find herself in the direct line of sight of none other than Michael.

Seven

Monica's smile faded as she stood for a moment in suspension. Michael . . . here? There was, however, nothing of the beat-pounding patrolman in the man across the room. This man was dressed with dark formality and stood with an ease and dignity that proclaimed his right to be here. There was a magnificence about him that was accentuated by the elegance of his tuxedo. Its crisp, white dress shirt brought out the bronzed tint of his skin, which in turn complemented the warm chocolate of his eyes.

His eyes. They seemed to be the only link to the Michael Shaw she'd known. Then she'd only suspected the extent of his refinement. Now it was as clear as the tiny dot of perspiration that had suddenly appeared on her nose.

"Uh, Craig?" She tore her gaze from Michael's to face her date once more. "Would you excuse me for a minute? I'd like to use the ladies' room."

He smiled agreeably. "Sure thing, Monica. I'll be waiting here. We can go in to dinner when you get back."

With a smile of thanks she escaped, grateful above all that Craig, in his own easygoing way, hadn't detected the subtle shock she'd experienced. *Michael . . . here?* She paced her steps carefully to counter the racing of her pulse. What was he doing *here?* Yes, she knew he had been a lawyer at one time. Goodness knew there were enough of *them* in the room tonight. Spotting the appropriate sign, she pushed against the door. And he'd mentioned "friends in high places" who had helped him find his waterfront condo. But . . . the *mayor?* Or was the connection another person here . . . perhaps the attractive brunette who'd been by his side just now. Oh, she hadn't missed *that!* Nor was the woman's identity a mystery. Monica had easily recognized her as Joyce Watkins, the city's renowned deputy mayor.

Standing in front of the wall-to-wall mirror

in the ladies' room, Monica glared at herself. Then, slowly, she forced a semblance of relaxation onto her features. Joyce Watkins was a good woman, bright and energetic . . . and married. So much for cattiness.

But Michael . . . *here?* She simply hadn't been prepared for this. He'd said nothing about his plans last night, but then neither had she. And their evening had come to an abrupt end with very few cordialities offered.

Opening her small evening purse, she extracted a tiny compact. Then she rested her hands on the counter and stared at herself in dismay. What was she going to do? Or rather . . . how was she going to *do* it? She had no choice but to go back to Craig and make the most of the evening. After all, the point of her being here was to chat with the visitors and pick up whatever information she could about new programs, old problems, shared dilemmas, and what have you. Unfortunately the only *what have you* in her own mind was Michael. How was she going to handle *that* for the evening?

Raising the compact, she dabbed her nose lightly, paused, and let her hands fall to the counter again. For a critical moment she looked at herself, trying to see what Michael might see. Yes, she was attractive. Not beautiful . . . despite what he might have mumbled in a daze of passion . . . but certainly appealing.

Much as Michael's shirt had done to his manly skin, her own white dress emphasized the light summer's tan she'd acquired. Her skin was smooth and soft, her bare arms slender. How often in the past she'd wished to be bigger-busted. Not tonight. The cut of her dress with its deep veed scoops both in front and back precluded the wearing of a bra. She'd believed the salesgirl, who'd told her how many women couldn't possibly wear this style. She could . . . and in her mildly biased opinion she looked well in it.

By the time her eyes reached their own reflection, her cheeks bore an added tinge of pink that was both becoming and feminine. She'd swept her hair up tonight, had loosely piled it to her crown, and secured it with a pearl-handled comb. The bangs worked well, she had to admit, giving her that softer look that Robert had strived for and Michael had noted so approvingly. Her bruises were healed now . . . but she'd keep the bangs anyway. She liked them.

But enough! Craig would send the troops in after her if she didn't hurry. The troops? With a moan of disgust at images that persisted in cropping up, she thrust the compact back into her purse, freshened her lipstick, and turned her back on herself. She could only buy so much time. Craig was waiting.

As it happened, so was Michael, standing tall and in animated conversation with Craig. Monica paused at the door for a helpless instant, wishing she had any other option but this. There was none. And Michael spotted her several seconds before Craig followed the line of his eyes. There was no escape. Willing herself to remain cool and calm, she took a deep breath and advanced.

"Monica!" Craig greeted her. "I'd like you to meet someone. This is Michael Shaw, a fellow I haven't seen in years. Mike . . . meet Monica Grant."

As Michael politely extended his hand her first question was answered. Were they to reveal that they knew one another? Evidently not. She extended her hand toward his, chagrined to find that its warmth and strength simply radiated innocence.

"How do you do?" he asked, deep velvet and smooth.

"Just fine, thank you," she responded, feeling suddenly bold and defiant. Two could certainly play the game! "Is it Your Honor? Are you a delegate to the conference?" Michael's eyes glittered, but it was Craig who spoke.

"No, no, Monica. Mike is in the city for

the summer as part of a law-enforcement project."

"Oh, he's in law enforcement?" she asked sweetly, eyes rounded.

"That's right," he answered in the firm tone she knew so well. "I'm on temporary assignment with the police department."

Craig leaned closer to Monica but spoke loudly enough for Michael to hear. "Your *favorite* topic. But go easy on him. He's a newcomer."

"He's gun-shy?" There was a deeper meaning to her gibe that only she and Michael understood. Craig seemed oblivious to the visual interchange between them, but he came to Michael's rescue nonetheless.

"This man gun-shy? You don't know who you're talking to."

Puzzled, she looked at Craig. In his innocence he was right. There was so much about Michael she didn't know. Perhaps this particular encounter, with Craig as moderator, was ideal for remedying the situation. "How do you two know each other?" she asked.

"We were in the service together. Mike was the one on the front lines. I wrote up the accounts of it. Despite the fact that it was a tragic war, it was still worth studying from a strategic point of view. Mike was part of a specialized commando unit. Green Beret."

It was a little more than she'd pried out of him in the past, and Monica felt a touch of satisfaction that Michael had grown more serious. She eyed him straight on. "I'm impressed. A war hero?"

"I wouldn't say that—" he began, only to be interrupted by Craig.

"I would! A Silver Star is nothing to sneeze at. Counterinsurgency work is tricky. Takes brains as well as courage."

"Then I'm particularly impressed." She tilted her head to one side, her eyes never once leaving Michael's. A coy smile played at the corners of her lips. "We were just going in to dinner. Why don't you join us?"

If she'd seen the discomfort in his eyes at the mention of his heroism, now Monica could almost see him squirm. The game she was playing could prove to be dangerous, but what did she have to lose? Michael had sworn off her last night. Perhaps it was her turn to recoup her losses and have a little fun into the bargain.

"Oh, I wouldn't want to intrude . . ." he said, looking from Monica to Craig and back. On the return trip his gaze picked up a taut-tethered sharpness, which he cast her way

for an instant before Craig's insistence settled the matter.

"Don't be silly, Mike. I'd like to talk with
you, hear about your work." *So would I,*
Monica thought with a smug smile. "Are you
with Joyce? Will she join us?"

Michael looked around to where the
deputy mayor was standing, involved in a
conversation several groups away. "Excuse
me. I'll check."

When he'd left, Craig turned to her. "I had
no idea Mike was in this area. He's a terrific
guy. You might even want to have him on
your show." She took in a breath of air the
wrong way and coughed as Craig went on.
"He may be a stranger to these parts but he's
got quite a reputation in the Midwest. He
worked as a lawyer for a number of years, a
prosecutor for—How about it, Mike?" he cut
off the thought just when Monica felt she
was getting her teeth into something at last.

But the man in question was approaching.
"She'll join us in a few minutes. Why don't
we go on in?"

For a fleeting moment, as they turned toward the buffet room, Monica had second
thoughts about the wisdom of this move.
Much as she might enjoy herself, and glean
a few kernels of information about Michael,
there was still the question of his proximity,

the physical appeal that never failed to touch her. But it was too late now . . . and it *had* been at her suggestion. Determined to make the most of it, she helped herself to a light selection of the gastronomic offerings and then followed Craig toward a small, unoccupied table. That Michael was right behind her she had no doubt. She could feel the awareness of him at the back of her neck, now open and exposed to his sight.

She was infinitely grateful for Craig, who took it upon himself to casually seat her and then engage Michael in conversation. At first she listened quietly, taking it all in as she picked at her Hawaiian chicken. Michael spoke about his work here, offering Craig a similar story to the one he'd told her. Craig seemed to accept it easily enough, though newsman that he was, he did have questions.

"I guess I've just been out of touch with you for too long. The last thing I heard you were making headlines as a federal prosecutor."

Monica's head came up too quickly for Michael to ignore it. "Is anything wrong, Miss Grant? You look troubled. Don't tell me you're opposed to *every* branch of law enforcement?" His smile was for Craig's benefit only.

"Me? Oh, no. It's Monica . . . and I was just wondering what Hawaiian chicken is doing at a thoroughly New England buffet. But, then . . . I suppose there are outsiders here. Where did you say you were from, Mr. . . . uh, Sergeant . . . uh, Officer . . . what *is* the proper form of address?"

"Michael." His arched brow, outwardly capping humor, held its own silent warning. "And I'm from Madison. Madison, Wisconsin."

"Originally?"

"No. I was born in Omaha."

"Ah." She nodded as though it explained everything, when in fact it was only a slight elaboration on that which she already knew. "A federal prosecutor? That must have been very challenging work. And great experience."

Still miraculously unaware of the undercurrent between the other two, Craig offered a further tidbit. "Mike was forearmed with experience going into that job. You served as state prosecutor for . . . five years?"

"Three."

"Okay," Craig went on. "Then it must have been after that later stint that I lost you. That was when you went with the police department?"

"That's right."

That's right. How many times had she heard him say those words? Offering no more, simply confirming what was stated by another. A clever man, this Shaw, she mused. "And in what capacity do you serve the police department . . . Michael?" she asked pertly. With Craig the Curious on her side she might make some headway.

But Michael chose his words carefully. "I worked mostly in the back room, behind the scenes."

"At the control center?" Craig interjected.

Michael's smile told him nothing. "There's a lot more to police work than the cop on the street, although one of the reasons I'm here this summer is to experience that side of it. Once I entered the Madison department at a higher level, it was hard to revert without causing an upset. Hierarchy and all."

Monica pondered his words, no longer considering the game she played, now only the content of what he'd said. "You make it sound so logical." She spoke thoughtfully, half to herself. Then fearing that Craig would think her comment strange, she quickly added, "You do have to admit that it invites suspicion to find a man as overqualified as you at the entry level of the department."

Again the raised brow, which this time quelled her imminent crack about his age.

"It takes a suspicious mind to make it an issue," he shot back softly. "The important things are that Boston has an extra man on the force, and that I have no complaints about it." He paused and she thought for a minute that he'd continue the farce by asking about her own occupation. He knew all too well how she felt about anonymity, and though he must have assumed it, he couldn't know for sure whether or not Craig knew the details. To his credit he turned instead to the other man.

"Tell me about you, Craig. I hadn't realized you were with Channel Seven . . ."

And so the conversation went, with Joyce Watkins joining them after a few minutes and very little other personal information being exchanged. The talk dealt mostly with politics and the upcoming gubernatorial primary in September. Monica participated readily, but was amazed at the extent of Michael's knowledge of the race. For a man who was simply visiting the city he'd picked up a wealth of background information. He *was* intelligent; she had to hand that to him. He was also gorgeous, sitting there as laid-back as he was, comfortable and at ease in his formal attire, handling Craig's occasional introductions to passersby with aplomb.

And then there was his jaw, ultrasmooth

and smelling oh, so faintly of after-shave. And his ears, skimmed at the top by the thick crop of spice-shaded hair. She could see more of the gray wisps now, gleaming in the light, adding stature rather than age. Then there were his fingers, long and straight, absently tracing the tines of the dessert fork that remained by his place.

As the minutes passed the strain increased. Monica struggled to devote her full attention to the conversation, but her eye wandered persistently. Surreptitiously . . . but persistently. She was thoroughly relieved when that last fork disappeared with a sit-down dessert, and it was time to meander through the crowd again.

"Monica, it was a pleasure meeting you." Michael offered his hand and a smile that was more perfunctory than cordial.

She was less composed, unable to produce even the ghost of that smile. "The pleasure was mine, I'm sure," she murmured. "Enjoy your evening." *And your summer.* The edict of last night was obviously in force. Michael had no use for her. He had not so much as asked her the simplest personal question.

It was much later, in the privacy of her apartment, that she realized how hurt she felt. He'd certainly played the role to the hilt, pretending not only that he didn't know her but, further, that he didn't care to know her beyond the most superficial level of a *how are you* or *a pleasure meeting you.*

This wasn't how it was supposed to be, she silently protested as she paced the length of her balcony, and back. As a hero Michael Shaw was a flop! He should have done *something*—whisked her off into the dark of the nearest alcove for an angry, if stolen kiss, tormented her with a wandering hand beneath the table during dinner, murmured a snidely seductive remark in her ear when Craig wasn't looking—*something!* He might have even complimented her on her dress without giving away their past. But to very calmly take her in stride?

In the final analysis she couldn't summon up any indignation. He'd done nothing. *Nothing.* She couldn't believe it after the passion they'd seemed to share. Evidently he would make good on his decision that she was more trouble than she was worth. And the only thing she could do was to forget him.

That was easier said than done, however, for the start of the week passed uneventfully—uneventfully and hence ripe for distraction. Then on the Wednesday evening show the pickpocket called again. It was a short call coming at the tail end of a discussion on the evils of old age, one of which, highlighted by the callers, was the fear of crime and the vulnerability of the aged.

Monica pushed a blinking button. "Hello, you're on the air."

"I know about crime and the elderly," said the same flat voice she'd heard once before.

"You do?" she returned less surely, glancing quickly over at her guest, the planner of a local retirement community. Not surprisingly he was unaware that this call might be any different from those that preceding it.

"Yes. The elderly are slower and therefore safer targets. They carry stuff on them—jewelry and all—so they won't be wiped out of a favorite item if their homes are robbed while they're gone. And their clothing is often looser fitting. It's simple to pick their pockets." There was a bit of the braggart in his tone, prompting Monica's probe.

"You sound as if you've had experience." She carefully tested the water. Last time she'd simply hung up on him, and it had bothered her for days. This time she'd try to see where he wanted to lead her.

"You might say that. For those of you out there keeping count, it was number thirty-two earlier tonight."

Thirty-one, over the course of three and a half months now, had taken place on Monday at the marketplace. Today thirty-two? "Whereabouts?" she asked, realizing that if the place he named could later be verified, they'd have a clue to whether he was telling the truth. He couldn't have learned anything from the newspapers, whose late afternoon editions would have already been on the stands and whose morning editions were a long way off. Perhaps he'd listened to a police band . . . or a news program might have mentioned it. She could check all that out later.

"Right in front of the Ritz," he stated proudly.

Monica could see Sammy's gestures beyond her glassed-in booth, but she persisted. "And what did you get this time?"

"A watch. A gold watch."

"Not bad. But"—she took the stab—"you didn't tell us your name. How can we identify you?" She held her breath.

"The pickpocket. That's all you need to know."

She opened her mouth to protest, but he'd hung up, leaving her to tie up the loose ends of the show in her sorry state of frustration. Sammy was waiting when she finally signed off, removed her headset, and left the booth.

"Good show, Monica! You can't believe

the number of calls we've gotten since that guy called."

"The pickpocket?" Now that the initial shock was over, thought of the thief made her think of Michael. "He's probably a fraud," she scoffed.

"He got the right place and the right article. One of those calls was from the police."

"Oh?"

"Donovan from District Four." Of course, she mused. Shaw would be off duty. "He confirmed the information, but he seems to think that the story's been carried on several news updates, both on radio and television. He's checking it out. But he wants to talk with you."

"What for?"

"Handling the guy if he calls again."

Monica felt suddenly full of her old resistance. "*You* talk with him, Sam. I'll talk with Ben Thorpe. He's the psychiatrist, and he's sure to know a lot more about this pickpocket's mind than Donovan." She wondered what Shaw would have to say, but it was a moot point, since she had no particular reason to speak with him. "On the chance that Donovan has anything of interest to add, you can pass it on to me. Hey . . . why Donovan? Or hasn't Salazar gotten through yet?"

Sammy gave her a knowing grin. "He got through, all right. Right after I spoke to Donovan. I told Salazar we'd deal with Donovan."

"And he didn't give you a fight on it?"

"Odd . . . he really didn't. Maybe someone up above has finally given the guy a warning . . . or a lesson in basic public relations."

Monica chuckled halfheartedly. "He needs a whole lot more than that." *Had* someone spoken to him? Did Michael have any part in the switch? Tired, she massaged an aching temple. "Well, I'm going to run, Sammy. Thanks for covering for me. I'll talk with you tomorrow?"

"Sure thing. Take care."

"I will." She smiled and she knew she would—physically. Psychologically she wasn't as sure. That night she thought of Michael, annoyed above all that she missed him. It was bad enough that whenever she passed a policeman or was passed in turn by a cruiser, she wondered if it was he. But now this small matter that related indirectly to the police had come up. The pickpocket—how could such a ridiculous little thief create such havoc? How could the man continue to elude the police? Hmmph! The answer to that should be clear, she mused. But it wasn't. Michael was sharp, and he claimed that there were others in the department whom he very much respected. Why wasn't Michael on this case? At least then she might be able to look forward to seeing him every once in a while, even if only for business. Or was that worse? She no longer knew. Last Sunday evening had been a torment. But it somehow seemed better than nothing at all.

Monica's frame of mind verged on the grumpy when she finally called Sammy the following afternoon. And his message, relayed from Inspector Donovan, did nothing for her mood.

"He wants to put a trace on the lines, Monica."

"*Our* lines?"

"Yup. Your show. He's sure the guy will try to call again, and if you can keep him on for a couple of minutes they might be able to—"

"No go, Sammy!" she exclaimed, irate. "They've been unable to catch him, so now they'll have us do their dirty work? I can't let them trace our calls! Do you have any idea what that would do to the other callers?"

"Take it easy, Monica. I told him we wouldn't, but the only good argument I have is that we've got no way of knowing for sure whether this is their man. Donovan did check it out, and the guy could have learned what he told you from radio news broadcasts. And Donovan claims that your audience doesn't need to know they've been bugged or traced."

"They'd find out one way or another—certainly if this one turns out to be the culprit and something positive turns up in the trap."

"But if something good does come of it, you'd be a hero anyway," Sammy argued, unaware that at her end of the line Monica winced at the term.

"Heroine," she corrected. "Please. And I won't do it. Not yet, at least. Besides, Ben feels that the fellow is troubled, whether he's the pickpocket or not. He needs the attention, and if we scare him off, he'll only look for some other outlet. Tell Donovan to wait. Or get his police cracking." She grinned factiously. "Tell him how wonderful his men would feel if they could catch the fellow on their own. Ego-boosting," she added curtly.

Sammy was quiet for several moments. "You'd never make it as a PR person either," he chided her gently. "The words are right— the tone is way off."

Her smile this time was genuine. "That's why I need you, Sam. You're a very precious shield." She winced again as she pictured Michael's badge, the chest it rested upon, the warmth within. Then she tossed back her head and took a breath. "I'll trust you to keep the hounds at bay. Now, as to more pressing matters, have you received that bio on the professor? If he's supposed to be on tonight, I've got to know something about him."

"Right here, Monica. Hold the phone. I'll read it to you."

The show went well, with no interruptions. Several callers made reference to the alleged pickpocket, but Monica was able to pacify them with any one of several noncommittal statements that she and Sammy had worked out beforehand. On Friday night, however, the man called again, this time in the midst of a segment on the Runaway Child.

"Hello, you're on the air," she greeted her caller unsuspectingly.

"Hi, Monica. It's me again." She'd recognize the voice anywhere but had forcefully put it out of her mind. Now she straightened up instantly.

"How're you doin'?" she asked, trying to think ahead.

"Just fine. Got a beautiful bracelet this afternoon."

She was right with him. "That was what the evening papers said. You'll have to tell me something I don't know! How else will I know for sure that you're our pickpocket?"

In the silence that followed Monica feared she'd lost him. She breathed more freely when he spoke, but only for a minute. "You play a mean game, Monica. But so do I. *I* was the one who ran into you that day. You remember? A couple of weeks ago? On Washington Street? I really didn't mean to but you got in the way. You see, the cops were on my tail, and I wasn't watching where I was going. I recognized you though. You didn't recognize me?"

It was as if the wind had been knocked from her all over again. This was a piece of information she couldn't pass off so lightly. "So it *was* you?" she asked. No one outside the police department had known about the incident. There had been no report to any branch of the media. He'd earned some credibility by virtue of this confession. Whether he was *the* pickpocket had still not been conclusively established.

"It was me," he admitted proudly before his tone turned meaner. "And I wouldn't go to the cops if I were you. I've been a fan of yours since you began. Let's just keep this between the two of us."

"But you're on the air—" she began, but he'd hung up. Shaken, she looked out at Sammy, took a deep breath, then pulled herself together. "For all of you out there who just heard that little call, let me remind you that our caller may be nothing more than a prankster. The incident to which he referred . . ."

After a brief explanation, which she felt she owed her listeners, she managed to return the discussion to the subject at hand. It was only when the show was over that she gave in to the briefest fit of trembling.

Sammy opened the booth door and leaned in, concerned by her pallor. "Are you okay, Monica?"

"Fine," she said quietly, remaining in her seat nonetheless and forcing herself to breathe deeply. "That was a shock. He knew about my accident!"

"He seems to know you pretty well. He said he recognized you right away. How could that be . . . if he only *listens* to the show?"

Puzzled herself, she shrugged. "I don't know, Sammy. I don't know."

"Maybe we should get the police in on this one."

"No!" Her head shot up. "Not yet!"

"What are you waiting for? He started sounding ugly at the end. Whether he's the pickpocket or not, I don't like it."

Monica pressed a finger to her brow and closed her eyes tight. "If he is the pickpocket, he's harmless. At least he has been up to now. And if he isn't the pickpocket, he probably doesn't have the nerve to do anything. He's had plenty of time between that knockdown on Washington Street and tonight. If he was worried I'd tell the police something, surely he would have gotten to me earlier."

At that moment an assistant called Sammy to the phone. He was back within a minute. "It's Donovan again. What should I tell him?"

Monica stood and gathered her things together. "Tell him no."

"I think you should—"

"No! Tell him, Sam . . . please?"

Her producer stared at her in frustration. "I could overrule you."

She stared back no less fixedly. "You could. I suppose it's your choice." Suddenly not wanting to know his decision, she hoisted her bag to her shoulder, lifted her briefcase, and made a deceptively calm exit.

However, tension flowed through every inner channel of her being. She felt keyed up and . . . and . . . in limbo. There. She'd said it. She hadn't meant it in as general a sense as Michael had that night, but regarding this specific moment in her life she did feel in limbo. It was as if she were waiting for something to happen. She was headed home, yet she felt aimless. She was off now for the weekend, yet she felt little enthusiasm for those days of rest and relaxation . . . alone. She had plans, a cookout to go to on Saturday night and a brunch cruise to take out on the harbor on Sunday. Both were gatherings of different groups of friends. Neither had any specific meaning other than a pleasant few hours spent with others. Last week, last month, last year, that would have been enough. After all, she had her work and this was play. Suddenly, though, she wanted something more.

As she made her way to the street and crossed to enter the Common she wondered what the pickpocket—or whoever her enigmatic caller was—had done to inspire this soul-searching. Perhaps nothing. Perhaps everything. Why was it that the fellow bothered her so? Or was it that he made her think of Michael?

She remembered with crystal clarity how Michael had knelt beside her that first day, drawing back her hair from her face, talking so gently to calm her. She remembered his washing her bruises, turning the pages of the mug shot book for her, kissing her. *Damn!* she muttered a curse into the darkness as her feet bore her on toward the center of the Common. Why was his image there, always there? How could he remain with her longer than any other man? What was so special about him? Unfortunately the answer to that was no mystery.

With an angry exclamation she stopped to readjust the shoulder strap which her punishing pace had caused to slip. Then she raised her head and listened. Had it been her imagination—that single footstep following her last one? Of course it had to be! Starting up again, she moved just as quickly, though with a less punishing impact to her step. *He* had put the bug in her ear. Michael had been the one to harp on the danger of her walking home alone at night along these paths. Was she now becoming paranoid?

To prove to herself that there was nothing to her fear, she stopped again. Again the echo. And that was all it was, she decided. An echo. But she walked faster still. It was absurd. Who would possibly follow her? She had no money on her, except for several dollars in her purse. She wore no expensive jewelry. And she refused to consider another motive besides robbery. Breathless, she stopped a third time. Granted her heart was thudding loudly against her ribs, but there was a step. Closer now.

Without any further thought she broke into a run, realizing she was more than halfway across, that the only way was to go on. The path was lit but very dimly, and the light fell off quickly on either side. If she were to yell, she would only be expending useless energy. Until she reached the far side of the Common, there would be no help. Where were the usual dog-walkers? And the patrols? There was no one in sight.

With a helpless glance back over her shoulder she caught sight of a dark figure. She ran on, quickly growing terrified, glanced back again to see the figure gaining on her. She could see nothing else except that he was large and obviously trying to overtake her. In the distance she saw the archway that led from the Common onto Charles Street. There were cars there. Someone might help . . .

She ran on, whimpering softly with every few steps, panting now and feeling the strain in every muscle. Soon she could yell . . . she was getting close enough . . .

Then a hand clamped down over her mouth, and as she thrashed wildly from side to side an arm clinched her waist to lift her off her feet. She struggled with everything left in her, but her assailant had purposely waited until the dash through the Common had taken its toll. She was no match for the strength that held her and the stamina that hauled her from the path and into the darkness behind a clump of trees. She tried to yell, but the hand that muzzled her deadened all sound as well.

She was held from behind, rendering her arms nearly as useless as her legs. She tried to bite but couldn't open her mouth wide enough. It seemed useless, and she was almost in a state of panic. *He'd* warned her! Why hadn't she listened? Where was he now that she needed him so badly? *Michael!* she cried, though no sound came out.

As she fought for her very life, she was dragged to the ground, and he was on top of her, his weight crushing her to the grass. It was dark, so dark. He had her pinned and positioned now, his hand still gagging her. She was his helpless victim, moaning frantically against imminent attack . . . or rape . . . or worse, murder . . .

Why did he wait? She steeled herself for the pain, but it never came. He did nothing but stare down at her, his back arched up off her chest, his hips anchoring hers to the ground. What was he waiting for? Or did he get his kicks feeling the panic that surged through her entire body?

Suddenly she heard his voice. *His* voice. It was somehow gruff and gentle at the same time. "Have I made my point?" he asked, rolling off her, removing his hand from her mouth, lifting her until she sat trembling and uncomprehending before him. "You wouldn't have had a chance, Monica. The damage would have been done by now."

"Michael . . . ?" she gasped in a bare whisper. It was too dark for details, and she was momentarily unable to move.

"Yes."

"Michael . . . ?" Again she gave a wisp of a voice to his name. Slowly, slowly she began to understand. It was stronger this time. "It was *you?*"

"Yes." With regret.

"*You* terrified me like *that* . . . to *make a point?*" she cried, but a crescendo had begun to mount within her, and her eyes widened in understanding. "*You* did that? How could you?" Still terrified but relieved, and growing more furious by the minute, she suddenly exploded, screaming as she'd been unable to do during the time she'd been struggling with him. "How could you do that to another human being? *How could you?*" Overcome with rage, she began to fight him then, hitting and pummeling him as she'd wanted to do when she'd first been dragged from the path. "Do you have any idea . . . what I felt? What I feared? What I thought? *Do you?*"

Michael let her pound away for several

moments, as though he welcomed the punishment. She was still crying out at him when he captured her wrists and pulled her against him. Arms around her back, he held her as she dissolved into racking sobs. "I've never . . . been . . . as . . . scared of anything . . . in my . . . life," she sobbed, only then realizing that she was actually safe.

His arms tightened around her. One hand stroked her back, then pressed her head more tightly against his chest. She thought she heard an "I'm sorry, love," but the rapid beat of his heart and her own continued weeping blotted out all other sound.

"Oh, Michael," she moaned a final time. "How could you have done that? I was so frightened . . ."

This time she could hear his voice clearly. It was soft and sorrowful, close by her ear. "I know, love. I know. Shhhh." He shifted his arms to hold her even more securely. "Everything's all right now. I'm sorry."

"Why did you *do* that?"

"I guess I had to prove something to you."

"But why . . . like that?" She relived a split second of terror and began to shake again.

"I was angry, I suppose. You're a very stubborn woman. You won't let us do anything for you. And I'm worried, Monica. I'm worried."

"You heard the show tonight?"

"In its entirety."

"And the pickpocket?"

"He knows you. He knows your face and your job. He operates in this area. For all you know, he could easily have followed you home any night this week. Doesn't that worry you?"

Monica sat back on her haunches, and Michael allowed her that much distance. He kept a hand on her shoulder, though, fingers curved around the back of her neck, and that she allowed. "I doubt he's done that. He wouldn't take the risk of discovery at this stage. I think he's enjoying himself too much."

After a moment's silence Michael stood up and brought her up with him. She could hear the edge to his voice. "Let's get out of here. We can talk back at your apartment."

It was the edge that reminded her of the weekend before. "You don't have to do that. Now that you've done your thing, you can leave me alone. I'm sure I won't be accosted a second time tonight."

But Michael's hand was gently insistent on her arm. "I had actually intended to walk you home from the studio from the start. You bolted out of there so quickly, though, that I had to run to catch up."

They were on the path now, and the overhead light illuminated his face. It was somber, his expression bearing no sign of victory. Monica's eyes were still moist. "You mean—your little joke was a spur-of-the-moment thing?"

His jaw clenched. "I hadn't intended it as a joke, and I'm sure as hell not laughing now. To be blunt, I was furious, and it seemed as good a time as any to show you how easily you could be victimized."

"Which you did very successfully!" She could still feel the terror, and she knew that it would be with her for a long time to come.

"*You* tell me that," he riposted in turn. But the thumb that wiped the tears from her cheek was almost timid. "Will you be more careful now—take a cab, get someone to drop you, let *me* walk you home?"

"I thought you wanted nothing further to do with me?"

He stiffened and dropped his hand. His gaze fell to the dark path, and in the faint light she saw deep furrows appear on his brow. "Yeah, well, that's what I have to talk to you about. That's why I came by for you in the first place."

A part of Monica knew that the smartest thing she could do was to declare she'd have nothing further to do with *him* and stomp off

with her head held high. In the first place,
however, she doubted she could stomp anywhere with her legs in the rubbery condition
they were in. In the second place, there was
that other part of her that wanted desperately to be with Michael. It was that part of
her that wanted to be woman to his man. She
simply couldn't deny it any longer.

"Talk?" she asked softly.

"For now . . . that's all."

"You won't up and storm off all angry
again, will you?"

"Not unless you set out to provoke me."

Each voice had softened in response to the
other. Monica marveled at her own docility,
particularly in light of the scare he'd given
her moments before. She should still be in-
censed. But she wasn't. Either she was losing
her fiery touch, she mused, or . . . or . . .

"All right," she murmured as she looked
up at him. The relief she saw, even in the
night's meager light, made the decision
worthwhile.

Michael's regard grew mellow then as
without another word he put an arm around
her shoulder and offered the support he must
have known she needed. They walked in silence until the Common was left behind and
the sidewalks of Charles Street beckoned.

"So much for karate," he teased her softly.

His hand tightened almost imperceptibly on her shoulder.

"I lied," she whispered.

"I know."

"It was worth a try."

"Hmmph! Maybe you *should* take lessons."

"Then I might have hurt you."

"You couldn't have hurt me. I'm—"

"—bigger and stronger? I know. I've heard that one before."

"Remember it!"

How could she forget it with that body walking in perfect step beside her? Up Charles to Mt. Vernon, then on to West Cedar. By the time they reached her apartment, the telephone was ringing. Michael unlocked the door and stood back for Monica to run ahead.

"Hello?" There was no response. "Hello?"

"No one there?" Michael had dropped her keys on the table and approached.

"No." She replaced the receiver. "Must have just hung up. If it was important, whoever it was will call back."

"Do you often get calls at this hour?"

She lifted her hair from her neck and went to switch on the fan in the living room. "Sometimes. My friends know when I get in.

Or if Sammy has something to say that he forgot earlier." Sinking into a chair, she rested her head against its back. In the wake of her trauma in the park she felt weak. She knew that Michael had joined her when his voice came from directly overhead.

"Are you all right?"

"Still shaky." She gave him a feeble smile, but her eyes were closed.

He touched her hair lightly, then went over to sit on the sofa. "I really am sorry, Monica. I wanted to put a good scare into you, but I guess I got carried away."

"That's for sure!" she cried, jerking her head up, her eyes open. But she grew quiet just as quickly. "Oh, Lord, I'm not up for a fight. You said you wanted to talk."

"I did. I—"

The telephone rang again. Monica hesitated, but at the quirk of Michael's head she rose to answer it.

"Hello?" she spoke evenly then, after a pause, with a touch of annoyance. "Hello!" The receiver met its cradle with greater force this time. "Damn!"

Michael was alert when she returned once more to the living room. "Same thing?"

"Mmmm." Who could it have been?

"Have you had the problem before?"

"No . . . well, no more than anyone. You know, wrong number here or there. I'm sure it's nothing."

Had it not been for the evening's ordeal and the fact that she still wasn't herself, she might have been aware of the subtle hardening of Michael's features. Now he stood up, thrust his hands into the pockets of his jeans, and faced her. "Look, maybe you ought to spend the night at my place. After that call from our friend tonight . . . and now this . . . it may just be that he knows your home number."

"It may just be that this is some other prankster. And besides, my home number's unlisted. He'd have to have connections somewhere to weasel it out of the phone company."

"Couldn't he get it from a mutual friend of yours?"

Catching at this strange thread of thought, Monica eyed him skeptically. "My friends wouldn't give out my number. Those who have it know why it's unlisted."

"What if our man is . . . a friend of a friend?"

"That's absurd, Michael!"

"Is it?" he replied, staring at her stonily. "Haven't you discussed the possibility that the pickpocket may live in one of the areas in which he operates? A caller to your show once suggested he might be 'one of us,' just out to cause a little mischief and have a little fun. What if he does know you . . . or knows who you are personally? What if he lives in *this* neighborhood?"

She stared at him, unwilling to accept the possibility. It *was* a possibility . . . but remote. "Oh." She shook her head slowly. "I don't think so. I'm sure he recognized me through . . . through . . . well I *do* go places once in a while, and it would be easy enough for someone to point me out. Last Sunday night, for instance. Anyone there could ask why *I* was there and learn who I was."

"That's just my point. Last Sunday night we were in an exclusive setting with an elite group of people. It may just be that our man is part of that group. It'd mean he's a particularly sick man. But think about it. It could be."

She thought about it. "I suppose," she admitted with a frown. When the phone rang again, she literally jumped.

"Let me get it," Michael moved.

"No! It's fine. I'll get it." But he beat her to the kitchen and had the receiver to his ear before she could stop him. Her reflexes were dull, she decided, by way of explaining her capitulation. She didn't want to face the fact that she was relieved to have him here to answer the phone . . . if nothing else.

"Hello?" she heard him bark, then a pause. "Who is this?" he demanded gruffly. Monica waited with her heart in her throat until he muffled the receiver against his chest. "It's a Jason Ward?"

Her eyes lit in instant relief. "Jason!" she exclaimed, quickly coming to the phone. "He's a friend," she explained as she took the receiver from Michael. "Jason, hi! . . . No problem . . . The party? . . . Sure. Tom can give me a lift . . . Of course not . . . Don't worry. You just go have a good time and I'll be in touch soon . . . Sure. Oh . . . and Jason?" She caught her breath. "Was that you trying to call a little while ago? . . . No? . . . Oh, nothing. The phone was ringing when I ran upstairs. That's all. . . . Okay. Take care."

When she turned around, Michael was staring hard. "Who is Jason Ward?"

"A friend," she replied, wondering whether this tension was suspicion or jealousy. "Just a friend. He was going to pick me up to go to a cookout tomorrow, but he's decided to go to the Cape for the weekend."

"You don't sound disappointed."

"He's a *friend*, Michael. The cookout is an innocent gathering of friends. One of the others can easily pick me up."

"Tom?"

"You *were* listening, weren't you?"

"There was always that chance your friend was our man."

"Jason?" she laughed. "Jason happens to be a brilliant newspaperman. He is also one of the clumsiest men I know. There's no way he could possibly pick anyone's pocket without fully alerting them in the process!"

Looking only mildly pacified, Michael nodded. "I see." He paused. "And it wasn't he who called before?"

"No." She waved off the earlier false alarms with a flip of her hand. "I'm sure those calls were nothing."

"I still think you should come home with me."

It was a mind-boggling proposal. Monica's face held the confusion she tried to deny with her words. "I couldn't do that. We both know what would happen . . ." As her voice trailed off she looked more poignantly at Michael. He stepped closer and touched the back of his hand to her cheek.

"Would it be so awful?"

She suddenly didn't know. That same fear was lurking within her, as it had been from the start. She felt unbelievably attracted to Michael. Yet they had so very many differences. Would one night be enough, and if not, how could she survive the constant turmoil to come?

"I'm frightened," she whispered, hardly knowing she had spoken at all.

He moved even closer. "Of what, Monica?" His hand seemed to lose itself in her hair, and she tilted her head up to him. His face was so close, mere inches away. The scent of him filled her nostrils, his warmth reached out to her. Her mouth felt dry . . . then lonely . . . and she only knew she wanted to kiss him.

"Of this." She gasped as she stood on tiptoe and brought her lips to meet his. She'd never initiated the kiss before, and she half-wondered if he would rebel. The traditional hero would insist on taking the lead. Once before she had suspected that Michael might not be as traditional as he seemed . . . just as he'd guessed that she was not as modern as the world believed her to be. Which was it— old-fashioned or modern?

Her lips moved softly over his, and she couldn't think anymore. As he opened his mouth to welcome her she let the kiss deepen. She felt his strength and was buoyed by it, sensed his desire and was encouraged. Her tongue explored the firmness of his lips, the even line of his teeth, the dark, moist interior of his mouth. With a sigh she wrapped her arms around his neck and brought her body flush against his. Then . . . the phone rang.

Gasping aloud, she tore herself away. It took the second ring to clear her mind. Breathing unevenly, she hesitated, then turned and ran to the kitchen. "Hello?" she croaked and cleared her throat. "Hello?" She heard nothing but her own quickened breathing. "Hello?"

Michael took the receiver from her hand, replaced it on its hook, and led her to her bedroom door. "Why don't you get some things together. I'd like you to come with me."

For an instant he could have been that same navy-clad patrolman, now gently taking her into custody. Monica's recollections of that first day flared up again, only to be tempered, then altered by everything that had taken place since. Michael Shaw was quite a man, uniformed or not.

With that small grain of conviction stored deep in her heart, she silently met his gaze. Fear of the intensity of her feelings was suddenly secondary to those feelings themselves. Without argument she did as Michael asked. Further debate was pointless. Oh, yes, there was that possibility that she had acquiesced out of fear, that she did believe herself to be in some kind of danger. More likely, however, she was going with him simply because . . . she wanted to go. She had reached the final chapter of *Passion's Challenge*. It was time now to see it through.

As for the epilogue, it remained as yet unwritten.

Eight

Having made the decision, Monica thought she knew what to expect. The twenty-minute walk from her apartment to Michael's, however, taught her otherwise. With each step the tension between them grew, and when they finally arrived at their destination she was vibrantly aware of how much there was about this man that she didn't understand.

His apartment itself was symbolic of her perplexity. It appealed to her instantly. Open and airy, in an even more contemporary style than her own, it was a stunning example of waterfront restoration, an ancient building preserved and rebuilt, with its original brick walls pierced by skylights and wall-to-wall windows. Of course, she reflected, someone else had found it for him before he'd arrived in the city, but still it was the last kind of habitat she would have picked for a cop. Of course, she mused further, he wasn't *really* a cop . . . just here for the summer . . . or was he? He'd been vague about so very many things.

Before her puzzled gaze, Michael let her broad-strapped overnight bag slip from his shoulder to the floor. She could see the tension in his back as he walked over to a sliding glass door, opened it, and disappeared into the night. Without a thought she followed him.

If her balcony was a grandstand for the traditional face of Boston, his offered a spotlight on its rebirth. Before them lay a panorama of lights and water, waving gently in the offshore breeze. This was the home port of *Old Ironsides*, the site of the Boston Tea Party so many, many years before. Yet it was delightfully modern now, with restaurants and high-rises acting in counterpoint to the refurbished wharves and walkways.

Monica gazed toward the backlit figure leaning on the sturdy wood railing. Who was he? Was he friend or foe?

"Some hero *you* turn out to be," she

teased him softly. "Now that you've finally got me in your lair, you turn your back and walk away from me."

His voice came low and troubled. "I shouldn't have brought you here."

"You said you wanted to talk," she reminded him, warily, though, and careful to keep a comfortable distance between them.

Straightening up, he drew a hand across his eyes. "There are so many things clouding the picture," he murmured, as though to himself, then, recalling her presence, turned back to her. "When I started out tonight, I knew we had to talk. I was angry last week—"

"You always seem to be angry at me."

She couldn't see his expression, but his tone was controlled. "There's a fine line between anger and other emotions. Tonight, for instance, I heard your show and felt this incredible need to protect you."

"So you attacked me instead?" Remembering that moment of sheer terror, she shuddered. It had been so real then. She had fully believed she was going to be cruelly hurt.

"That was unplanned."

"Not premeditated, therefore innocent?"

"Let's say that it was done on an irresistible impulse."

Monica shook her head. "You *are* the lawyer, aren't you?" she asked, knowing he must have been stupendous in the courtroom, wondering again why he'd moved to another arena. But he grimaced at the reference and turned away again. She refused to let him go as easily. "Why *do* you want me here? You've told me how much trouble I am. Why did you come after me tonight?"

The air was heavier, lightened only by distant city sounds, softened by the lap of water against the waterfront pilings. Michael seemed to be battling his own demons, head bowed, hands buried in the back pockets of his jeans. At that moment some protective instinct in Monica surged upward. She ached at his unhappiness, wanting only to ease it. No other man had ever evoked this kind of compassion.

Daring to come to his side, she put a hand timidly on his arm. "Why, Michael?" she asked softly, just beginning to realize the depth of her own emotional involvement. "I have a right to know."

His head swung around. "*What* right?" he shot back. "Or is this the feminist talking? Woman power?"

Stung by his bitterness, Monica recoiled. Then, as her own anger flared, she faced him. "You know, Michael Shaw, you're a bullheaded man. You ask me to understand your work—work that I detest—and I'm actually trying to understand. But when it comes to *my* feelings as a woman—a modern woman—you refuse to accept that there may be something worth understanding. We're not all *that* bad!"

"Oh?" he growled. "I'll take an old-fashioned girl in my bed any time."

"Passive? Is that what you want?"

"I want sweet and warm and receptive."

"But what about active and curious and eager?" she countered. "Can't I want your body as much as you want mine? Don't *I* have the right to express myself sexually—rather than just being there for you to express your needs?" Monica's voice had risen in pitch until Michael couldn't miss her anguish. Its intensity gave him pause.

"Is that what you're looking for—self-expression?"

She shook her head in dismay, then spoke more quietly and with a certain sadness. "You make it sound totally isolated and self-centered. I don't want to express myself for expression's sake alone. That's where you're wrong. If you were hurt once by your ex-wife, I'm sorry. But I am not her. I don't go around 'expressing myself' with every man I meet. Among other things, there's a critical matter of self-respect involved." After a gulp of air she barreled ahead. "As it happens, I haven't been with all that many men in my life. Good men are hard to find. And I happen to be very, very fussy. When I offer myself to a man, it's because I feel something here"—she pointed to her heart—"as well as here"—and her head—"and . . . Oh, what the hell!" She turned away and stormed off toward the living room, feeling hurt and humiliated once again, and devastatingly empty. "You wouldn't understand. You're too much of a pigheaded chauvinist who thinks a woman works best on her back."

A hand clamped on her arm and whirled her around. "That was a bigoted remark if I've ever heard one."

"You earned it!" she scoffed and tried to pull away.

"And just where do you think you're going?" he growled, but there was less anger now and the slightest hint of humor.

"Home! I shouldn't have come here. It was *my* mistake for wanting to be with you." Freeing herself, she made it halfway across the living room floor before he caught at her shoulder. She winced as he overtook her and swept her firmly into his arms.

"You're not going anywhere."

"Let me go!"

But he was looking at her almost gently now, and her argument suddenly lost its punch. "I love it when your eyes glitter like that," he murmured, his own shining warmly.

"You're a bully," she countered, but without conviction. His gaze had begun a slow tour of her features. Her stomach fluttered, her knees felt weaker. Neither had anything to do with the scare she'd had earlier that night.

When he spoke, there was only tenderness in his voice, his face, his arms. "If I'm a bully, it's only because I want you so much. I tried to stay away. I gave it a full week this time. But I need you, Monica. God, how I need you," he ended hoarsely. Then he kissed her, and she forgot all but his needs and her own. Every bit of the uncertainty that had plagued her no longer seemed important. The only thing that mattered was being in the arms of this wonderfully strong and tender man.

Arms clinging to his back, she returned his kiss, translating spirit into passion with every ounce of her femininity. It felt so right to seek his body for support, to open her lips for the plunder of his tongue, to strain against him with this hunger that only he could stir and sate.

He held her back for a breathless moment, and she knew he had as little patience as she did. "Come on," he whispered, taking her hand and leading her into the bedroom, where he switched on a dim bedside lamp and threw back a gray-patterned quilt. Monica saw nothing about the room save the tall, handsome man who dominated it. A wildfire licked at her nerve ends, spread through her veins until her heart was beating to a frenzied tempo.

Michael came to her then and cupped her face in his hands. His lips parted hers for a hot intermingling of gasps and sighs and cries of desire.

"Ahhh . . . Michael," she whispered, "I need you too!"

He crushed her pliant body against his firmer one for a minute, moaning his sweet torment into the warm cloud of her hair. "Monica," he rasped, "if I were . . . able to . . . I would undress you slowly piece by . . . piece. But I don't . . . think I can . . ." She could feel a tremor pass through the muscles of his arms and through his torso. "I need you . . . right now!" She could feel that too, and it excited her all the more. Catching her breath, she looked up at him.

Then, by mutual, silent consent, they allowed an arm's width between them. Fingers worked frantically at buttons and belts, mixing here and there, moving from one body to the other. A shirt and a blouse fell to the floor, then two belts, one wide, one narrow. Then their hands tugged at snaps and buttons and zippers, again working back and forth and between short, fiery kisses. Monica kicked off her sandals, pushed her slacks down and off, then stood to watch as Michael tossed his jeans carelessly aside.

"Come here, love," he said, but she was already in his embrace, coiling her arms around the sinewy column of his neck as he unhooked her bra and pulled it from her. Then he lifted her against him, and she cried out at the beauty of their bodies' fit. Together they fell back to the waiting sheets for a fevered kiss before each wrestled the other's remaining underthings from long, heated limbs.

Monica had never experienced this kind of all-consuming need. She reached for him, and he linked his fingers through hers as he lowered himself over her. When his bare flesh met hers, she thought she would explode. Crying out his name, she arched against him. He kissed her deeply, breathlessly, until neither could stand the agony of separation any longer. Then he ended it.

With the flex of his back and the reflex of

his hips he entered her. "Monica . . . !" he sighed. "Ahhh . . . love . . . so warm . . . rich." He had paused for a brief moment to savor the sensation fully.

She felt him, full and electric, charging her even in those quiet instants. "I need you, Michael," she breathed, raising her head from the pillow to seek his lips. Then he began to move, and the sounds of satisfaction burst from her throat and his in unbroken harmony. When he released her hands, she touched him, running her palms along his length from thigh to shoulder. His skin was firm and manly, his contours lean and muscular.

Everything about him excited her, from the way his superior height protected her and his bodily strength caressed her to the way he merged with her, deeper and deeper, gently and knowingly and then, with raw and untethered virility.

Then the details were lost to her. She heard his voice praising her, coaxing her. She smelled the rare beauty of him. She felt his movements quicken as her own mirrored their bodies' urgency. She knew of a rising, a spiraling, an imminent eruption. And then she was aware of nothing but a glorious mutual ecstasy, a suspension that lingered, lingered for what seemed an eternity before gently shimmering its way back to reality.

Michael's body slowly collapsed, and he rolled over on his side, pulling her over with him. His breathing was ragged, yet his arms possessed amazing strength when they tightened to hold her against him. "I knew, Monica . . ." he moaned, his lips against her hair.

"I know," she whispered back. She had sensed it too, long ago. For, whatever the cause, their lovemaking was destined to be spectacular. It was in part what she had feared, this taste of heaven. Life would surely pale in comparison to the ultimate joy she'd just experienced with Michael.

As she caught her breath against his chest, she felt a moment's panic. Her arms slid more tightly around his back, and she wished never to have to let go. Inevitable as their parting was, she simply couldn't face it now.

His voice came, deep and husky. "I doubt they'd have done it that way in a typical romance."

"No?" She let her head fall back against his arm, satisfied that their bodies were otherwise intertwined. His face was magnificent in the wake of passion. His hair fell rakishly over his brow, his skin was dark and damp, his eyes bore the light of fulfillment, making her tingle again.

"Your hero would have taken it slowly," he declared. The corners of his lips twitched, and she put her own to them for an impulsive moment.

"Oh?" Her own smile was one of happiness.

"That's right. He would have seduced you properly, tormenting you with his utter self-control until you were writhing beneath him, begging him to possess you. And you"—he grinned, inching his hand along her hip—"would have been prim and protesting right up to that last moment of abandoned pleading."

Monica gave him a mocking frown. "You've been listening to stereotyping reviewers. Anyone who's up on the field knows that there's the contemporary side to it too. Yes," she conceded, "it would certainly have been more drawn out, but there are some heroines who would have *you* writhing—"

"Ah," he quipped, "the liberated woman . . ."

Her brow puckered as she reflected on the term. Michael had just made love to her in the most traditional of ways. He had taken the lead and known instinctively what pleased her. She wouldn't have dreamt of having it otherwise. Their coming together had been combustive.

"Would you have let me . . . ?" she began, unsure but curious on principle.

"Let you what?"

"Let me . . . take the lead?"

"Tonight? No." Then he faltered. "And don't call me a chauvinist again. You have to understand, Monica. Part of what I needed was to take the reins, to command your satisfaction. I don't think of it as a selfish thing. But part of my fulfillment is knowing I've engineered your pleasure. Is there anything wrong with that?"

She pondered his words, leaning forward to lightly kiss the warm hairs on his chest. "No. You always have a way of saying it that makes it sound right." She kissed him again on that same spot, drawn back by the manly tang of his skin. "But can't I enjoy that privilege once in a while?" Leaning away from him, she allowed herself to look at his body for the first time. "Your body is . . . beautiful," she whispered in awe.

"You've seen that many?" he asked with a teasing growl.

"Of course not! But yours . . ." She put her fingertips on his waist then slowly moved them lower. ". . . yours turns me on . . ." In that instant she realized she wanted him again. Her insides were throbbing with reawakening desire. Looking quickly up at him, she asked the silent question. But Michael wanted to hear her speak her need for him.

"Tell me what you want, love," he gently urged her.

"I want to pleasure you, Michael. I want to touch you and know you. I want to show you what I mean when I say that you excite me."

Stealing her line, he looked at her tenderly. "You have a way of saying it that makes it sound right. But what about me, love? I can't just lie back and be still. That 'turning on' is a mutual thing, you know."

"I know." She grinned mischievously. Her hand was in a knowing place. "Oh . . . Michael," she moaned then, needing to be kissed more than anything. He accommodated her with a soul-reaching embrace.

What occurred then was a delightful compromise. Lying on their sides, each explored the other with a thoroughness that sent their shared pulses careening. Michael's man-rough hands traced the smoothness of Monica's curves, caressing her breasts and her belly, stroking that lower softness. In turn she explored the broad span of his chest, his narrower waist and hips. She reveled in the feel of him beneath her fingers, in her palm.

And he came alive at her touch just as he brought her to flame once more.

This time was slower, that typical romantic encounter where the tension built up and up to a point of exquisite desire, which then hurled them toward oblivion. But there was nothing of fiction in Michael's body nor in Monica's response to it. For this was no storied hero. This was Michael, and Monica surrendered her soul to him.

They slept at last in each other's arms, exhausted but totally fulfilled. When Monica awoke, it was to find her head resting against the warm pillow of his chest. Her legs were entwined with his. With each breath's fractional movement she was aware of his sandy-haired texture. His arms encircled her, one beneath her shoulders and around her back, the other resting over her hip. She had never known such a feeling of security.

Dawn had just begun to break, casting its pale blue light into the room. At some point during the night Michael had switched off the light and drawn up a sheet to cover them. Now the sheet was bunched low on their hips.

Yielding to temptation, Monica tipped her head back to look at Michael's features in repose as she'd never seen them. His head lay sideways on the pillow, his hair mussed, his cheek shadowed by a beard. She craned her neck to kiss his chin, then hesitated, fearful of waking him. But it seemed the damage had already been done.

With a deep, deep breath he started to stretch. Then he opened one eye to gaze down at the softly feminine form beside him. Tightening his arms around her reflexively, he opened the other eye. And very slowly a morning-after smile spread across the firm line of his lips. Monica returned it.

"Hi," she whispered.

"Hi."

"How did you sleep?" Still a whisper. It seemed wrong to break the morning's freshness with sound.

"Never better. How about you?"

She smiled against his chest. "The same." Shutting her eyes, she nestled closer, savoring the steady beat of his heart and the simple knowledge of his nearness.

"Monica?"

"Hmmmm?"

"You know what I'd like to do?"

Propping her chin on his chest, she looked into his eyes. They sent warm messages to her toes. "What?"

"I'd like to take off—just take off—and drive up along the coast. I haven't seen much of the North Shore or any of New Hampshire and Maine. I'd like to drive as far as Boothbay Harbor, taking my time, exploring and eating my way along. What do you think?"

"I think you'd never make it back before sundown."

"I had no intention of coming back." He shifted her onto her back and propped himself up on an elbow. "Come with me, Monica. We can take that drive and really relax. We'll find some place to spend the night, maybe in Boothbay itself. Then we can drive back tomorrow." There was an urgency to his invitation that went far beyond any sexual drive. She understood it intuitively. It was a spur-of-the-moment chance to escape their differences by leaving their workaday identities behind and going off together. She could think of nothing more enticing than the thought of having Michael all to herself for two days.

"I'd like that—oh, no, I've got plans!"

"Change them."

As she looked up at him she knew she'd change almost anything rather than give up an opportunity that might never come again. It was shortsighted and selfish. But it was what she wanted.

"I'll make my calls," she whispered, lifting a hand to comb the hair away from his brow.

Her fingers found root in that lush fullness, and she drew his face down for a kiss.

It didn't stop there. Could it ever? she asked herself later. In the process of that kiss Michael took command, holding her on her back while his lips and tongue explored her stirring body. Pinned to the sheet, she could only gasp and strain when his teeth closed gently around her nipple and his tongue darted across its pebbled peak. She could only sigh her pleasure when he nibbled his way to her waist and across her belly. His hands released hers when he moved lower, and still she couldn't move, held now by the branding tongue that seared the soft insides of her thighs, now by the fingers that tenderly stroked her. Then he found the center of her warmth and kissed her long and deep. She called out his name as her body arched, trembling, and sucked in her breath when it exploded.

It was only later, when he'd slid upward once more, that she could control her voice again. "What you do to me, Michael!" she gasped, her heart thudding wildly against his protective hand.

"No, no," he murmured softly. "It's what you do to me. I feel as though I've finally found my purpose in life."

"As a lover?" she asked in amusement.

His penetrating gaze overpowered her as his lips and fingers had done moments before. "As *your* lover," he returned intently.

Monica stared at him until her eyes filled with tears. Then she rolled over to bury her face against the pulse-point at his neck. "Oh, Michael . . ." she sighed, unable as yet to accept and name her emotion. "Michael . . ."

He held her until she regained control, then settled her beside him once more. Monica knew she needed time to assimilate the reality of Michael, just as she sensed he would have to reorient himself. Perhaps the weekend would be good for them both.

It was, beginning with the full breakfast of bacon and eggs and toast and home fries that Monica took delight in whipping up for him once they'd returned to her apartment. She made her calls, then repacked her overnight bag with a bathing suit and a fresh change of clothes. Then they headed out over the Mystic River Bridge in Michael's sporty BMW, leaving the city and its worries far behind.

Taking the shore route, they stopped in turn at Marblehead, Gloucester, and Rockport, wandering around the harbor shops, enjoying the summer air. At last they lunched on lobster stew overlooking an ocean dotted with pleasure craft.

Then they moved northward toward Newburyport, where they ambled along cobblestone streets before crossing into New Hampshire. They paused in York Harbor, on the southern flank of Maine. There they walked the beach hand in hand, delighting in the carefree feeling that came with the roaring breakers and the ocean breeze. It was cleansing in so very many ways.

For Monica saw the man as he was at that moment, unsullied by either past or future. He was right beside her, in the flesh, and she felt inextricably bound to him.

When they reached Kennebunkport, they strolled through blocks of quaint shops and galleries, admiring everything, needing nothing—nothing except the other's company. As they explored the beach further on, Monica knew a feeling of contentment that went far beyond physical repletion. As though reading her mind, Michael turned her into his arms.

"Are you happy?"

"I am."

"Glad you came?"

"Yup."

"What would you like to do now?"

"I don't know." She shrugged innocently.

"You're the one who's never seen the coast. Should we be heading on toward Boothbay? If we want to reach it and find a place—"

Michael kissed her. "I'm not sure I want to reach it after all," he murmured against her lips, just loud enough to be heard above the surf. "Right now I think I could use a bed . . ."

"You're a rogue," she taunted, but he wasn't the only one feeling the urge. Monica couldn't have cared less if she saw nothing but the naked length of Michael's body for the next twenty-four hours.

As it happened she settled for twelve. Michael miraculously found them a small cottage on the beach, where he held her captive, undressed and in bed, for all but the hour they took to eat out much later that night. He was as masterful a lover as he had been the night before . . . and then some. As if he were more secure now that they were away from Boston, he gave her free rein and reveled in it himself. He was everything she'd ever wanted, ever dreamed of—warm and understanding, dominant, then yielding as Monica was inspired. She had never spent so blissful a night. When morning came, she didn't want to move.

"Just a little longer," she protested when Michael hauled himself out of bed and stretched unself-consciously. When he turned to her she feasted on the vision of him. If he had been gorgeous in uniform and dazzling in jeans and shirt, he was absolutely breathtaking wearing nothing at all. Without a bit of embarrassment she promptly told him so.

"I love your body," she said quietly.

"That's a start. But I think I kinda guessed that last night." His fingers were long dark streaks against the paler skin of his hips.

She smiled. "You were very indulgent. Did it bother you?"

"Not at all."

"See? I told you there was something in it for you."

"Feel pretty smart, don't ya?"

She gave a pert shrug, looked up at him, and her eyes were entranced all over again.

"Monica, I'd be careful if I were you . . ."

"What's wrong?"

"Nothing's *wrong*. But I really think we should get going."

"Aren't we going for a swim?" She studied the pale outline that would be concealed by his bathing suit. "You promised me we'd have time before we left."

"We would have if we hadn't slept so late. Monica . . . look at me . . ."

"I am!" she cried, then shifted her gaze to

his eyes. Her own held a light that belied any wish to swim. Michael glared at her for a minute before he too surrendered.

"Ah, hell!" he groaned, reaching out for her and taking her with him down onto the bed. "It would be pretty embarrassing to try and put my trunks on now anyway." To her delight it was an understatement.

Much, much later that night, when she was back in her apartment and alone, she realized how much in love with Michael she was. It was the last thing she wanted, and it seemed hopeless, but it was undeniably true. The weekend had been pure heaven from those moments of ecstasy in Michael's arms Friday night to the last warm embrace before they'd gotten into the car for the return trip Sunday afternoon.

The tension had begun to grow with each passing mile. As Boston loomed up in the distance it was nearly tangible. Michael seemed to withdraw into himself, but Monica grew too preoccupied even to notice. When the BMW came to a halt outside her apartment, there was a hint of tragedy in the air.

"Look, Monica, I didn't want to argue while we were back up north, but I don't know if you should stay here."

"I told you—"

"I know what you told me. But I'm worried nonetheless. That pickpocket mentioned that you didn't recognize him. That could be interpreted to mean that you *should* have, that you *do* know him."

"That's ridiculous—"

"But it's possible. And I do agree with Donovan. The lines to the station should be tapped."

"You've spoken with Donovan?"

"Yes."

"No, Michael! I don't want to do that."

"You're being stubborn."

"You bet I am. When it comes to protecting the privacy of my callers I'll be very stubborn. They give only the minimum identification and know that their privacy will remain inviolate. I'll lose all my credibility. I can't betray their trust."

"What about your duty as a citizen?"

"What about it?"

"Don't you have a responsibility to cooperate in an investigation to nab a public pest?"

"That's all he is, Michael. A pest! Don't you see, he may have stolen things from coats or pockets or even wrists, but he hasn't quite proven to be a violent criminal!"

Michael's eyes had been harsh then, reminding her of everything he was, of everything she had detested for so many years. "It may be simply a matter of time. Can we afford to wait?"

Nine

There was little waiting to be done. The news greeted an already discouraged Monica when she arrived at the station for the Monday night show.

"Have you heard?" It was Sammy.

"Heard what?" she emerged from her silence to ask.

"It's manslaughter now."

"What is?"

"The charge against your friend the pickpocket. His latest victim had a heart attack on the scene. Dead on arrival at Boston City."

Comprehending and appalled, Monica's eyes widened. "My God, no!"

Sammy was as dour-faced as she'd ever seen him. "I'm afraid it's true. Right in the middle of the lunch crowd in the Public Garden. You didn't hear the news?"

She hadn't heard much of anything today, had barely been able to prepare for her show. She shook her head, still stunned.

"And . . . Monica . . ."

She held out a silencing hand. "I know, Sam. It's your decision." She turned away and retreated into the sanctity of that room she could call her own during those few minutes before going on the air. The phones would be tapped, if not tonight then certainly by tomorrow, when the police and the phone company would have had plenty of time to do their thing.

The police. Michael. Mention of his name brought a gnawing ache to her insides. She had no idea when she'd see him again. When he'd left last night he'd been angry . . . as usual. How could he have been so impatient—after the wonder of the weekend? He too must have been affected by their return to the city. Within its limits Monica was the liberated woman and Michael the street-prowling patrolman. In these capacities they seemed so far removed from one another.

Not for the first time did she stop to analyze her own behavior. Liberated woman?

Perhaps in some respects. But where had her spunk gone? With any other man she might have forced a confrontation, bluntly asking when she'd see him again, perhaps even asking where she stood in the scheme of his life. But she'd never loved a man like Michael.

It wasn't that she felt intimidated. She had too much self-confidence for that. Rather she was frightened—frightened that he might see her as nothing more than stimulating summer companionship. She'd known he was lonesome, that he wanted her company. But was she simply an expedient? After all, she reasoned, he would be leaving by Labor Day.

"Monica?"

She swung around. "Yes, Sam?"

"Your A segment just arrived. Should I set him up with a cup of coffee until you're ready . . . Are you feeling all right?"

"I'm—I'm fine. If you can keep him occupied for another five minutes, I can go over some last-minute notes."

"You look tired."

"I am." What could one expect on four hours of restless sleep? "But I'll be okay. Once we get going."

Indeed she was all right, and the show went along smoothly. If she'd been asked about its content afterward, she might have faltered in response. She only knew that she staunchly avoided all mention of the pickpocket, the police, and the tragic death in the Public Garden. Mercifully the culprit didn't call.

Distressed and weary, she emerged headdown from the Harper Building, intent only on getting home and into a hot bath as quickly as possible. Tension and the weekend's exercise had taken their toll on her overworked muscles. The resulting dull ache brought its own grief.

"Monica!"

Her head flew up with a start and she gasped. "Michael! You frightened me."

His expression was lost in the cover of night. "Better here than in the middle of the park."

She flinched at the recollection, then forced herself to walk quickly onward. As she'd fully expected, he was right beside her. "My bodyguard."

"Self-appointed." His voice was cool and even.

"You really don't have to do this," she began softly. "I think the only one I have to fear in this place is you." Her heart thudded at his nearness yet ached at his remoteness. Oh, yes, that was definitely there. He neither

touched her nor offered gentle words to recall their closeness. They were two different
people now, all the more awkward in contrast to that intimacy. She wanted to cry and
walked all the more quickly to combat the
urge.

He spoke with quiet conviction. "I told
you that I didn't want you walking home
alone."

"And I told you that I could take care of
myself."

"The other night didn't teach you anything?"

"That was you—not some rapist," she spat
out, putting every bit of her frustration into
the argument. Perhaps this *was* better, she
mused. Maybe if they fought whenever they
were together, she might learn to hate him. It
was a remote possibility, but worth a try.
Anything was better than loving and suffer-
ing alone. And since they did seem to be on
opposite sides of the fence . . .

"He's dangerous, Monica."

"So I heard." Though she kept on looking
straight ahead, she was aware of his scrutiny
beneath every lamppost. Her legs were
tired, but she rushed on.

"And it doesn't bother you?"

"I can't be worried about everything. He's
never made so much as a threat!"

"We're putting a trace on the phones tomorrow morning."

"Slow work. I thought you'd have them on by tonight." Thank goodness. Charles Street in sight.

"You're in a great mood."

"I'm tired and it's late. All I wanted was to walk home in peace."

He didn't say another word. Nor did he budge from her side until she'd reached the top of the stairs and unlocked her apartment door. Then, with a terse "Good night, Monica," he retraced his steps, leaving her to collapse against her door in bewilderment.

Once again he'd broken with tradition. Had this been a novel he would have pinned her to the door and angrily kissed her, punishing her stubbornness with the force of his mouth. He might even have swept her into his arms and carried her struggling to the bedroom, then dropped her unceremoniously and made violent love to her. . . . But he hadn't. She released her breath with a mixture of disappointment and despair.

If only she'd been less proud, spoken more gently. Perhaps she might have been able to get through to him. But what was the point? It seemed hopeless.

The hot bath she'd promised herself did little to ease her inner anguish. Nor did the warm milk help her sleep. Despite her fatigue she continued to brood. Muttering a choice expletive, she bolted from bed, grabbed *Passion's Challenge*, and made for the balcony. There she read its conclusion—and felt worse than ever. She had seen it through, had known the furthest reaches of rapture. Where did that leave her now?

Tormented by a nagging emptiness, she offered herself all the reasons why she was best estranged from Michael. They had conflicting opinions and divergent life-styles. It would never have worked anyway. Or would it? It was this germ of doubt that tore at her most. For the first time she almost believed she'd be willing to alter her life to fit a man's. For a liberated woman she mortified herself. But the fact remained that one part of her would follow Michael to the ends of the earth if it meant experiencing his warmth and gentleness, his intelligence and compassion again. Was she, after all, the old-fashioned girl Michael had pegged her for?

All her introspection was for naught. Michael didn't share her feelings. He certainly didn't love her. *She* was the only romantic of the pair, she mused, as she returned to bed and buried her face in the pillow.

Sleep was a stopgap measure. The next

morning found her as tense as she'd been
the night before. After spending several
hours doing research at the library, she
yielded to the urge for company and stopped
in at the law office of a friend to drag him to
lunch. That too failed to cheer her up.
Michael was still on her mind.

The situation was far from being remedied
when she returned to her apartment and
found a long white box propped prettily below her mailbox, with her own apartment
number scrawled in large black numerals on
its label. Flowers. He'd sent flowers!

Sweeping the box up into her arms, she
ran up the stairs toward the privacy of her
living room to open Michael's peace offering. Perhaps it had been a matter of pride
with him as well, she reflected as she tore at
the deep red ribbon that bound the long box.
Perhaps he too had been soul-searching
through the night. As she pulled off the box
top and more gently folded back thick layers
of tissue, her eyes flooded.

A dozen roses. Tall, slender, delicate, yet
still white and innocent. An old-fashioned
gesture—and she loved it! She closed her
eyes against the tears and bent low to inhale
the sweet smell of the buds. How forgiving
she could be, she mused as she chased
every angry thought from mind. When she

straightened up and reached out to lift the
roses, her hand found the card tucked between the thorns. Removing it carefully, she
read it . . . and frowned.

To Monica Grant, it said. *I really do enjoy
your show. Keep up the good work.* It was
signed, *An ever-loyal fan.*

Not Michael then, but an ever-loyal fan.
Whoever could *that* be? Disappointment
flooded through her, curbed only slightly by
perplexity. She'd tried to keep a low personal profile, but now a fan—who for some
reason chose not to identify himself—knew
both her real name and her address. Could
this have been her mystery caller of the other
night? But why wouldn't he give his name?

Disconcerted and strangely uneasy, she
stood motionless, the flowers in their box
still on the sofa, the card gripped tightly in
her hand. When the buzzer rang, she started
in alarm. Should she answer it? It might be
this fan come to see if she liked his gift. But
the last thing she wanted—or was in the
mood for—was to have to pacify a starry-
eyed admirer.

Then she paused. What if it was the post-
man? Or the UPS man? Hadn't her mother
said she was sending a package? Eyes round
in confusion, she glanced toward the door as
the buzzer sounded a second time.

Mustering the remnants of common sense, she peered out the window. If it was mail or a package, there would be a truck out front. There was no truck, though. Simply a black-and-white cruiser.

He'd come in person . . . even better than a gift! He'd come to apologize. Then she caught herself. No, he hadn't. Perhaps he only wanted to prolong the argument. He'd been so curt last night. Amid resurgent anger, she grew defensive. Why *had* he come?

The buzzer was on its third ring when she finally made it to the intercom button. "Yes?" she said, then cleared her throat to issue a more forceful "hello?"

"It's me, Monica. Buzz me in."

His order stirred her resistance. "What is it, Michael? I'm busy."

"I have to talk to you."

She hung her head, took a steadying breath, and realized she was being foolish. Even *had* he been the one to send flowers, he was a cad. But he was a determined cad, and he'd find one way or another to talk to her. Defeated, she pressed the button. It was only when his knock came and she reached for the knob that she recalled the card in her hand. Lunging to thrust it between the magazines in a nearby pile, she straightened her sundress and opened the door.

Michael was in uniform, as tall, dark, and handsome as ever. He even wore his hat—unusual—but then, she reflected wryly, he wouldn't want her to forget just who he was. Beneath the visor his eyes pierced her makeshift composure. "It took you long enough to answer the bell."

Were you worried? she wondered, but she knew differently. "I was in the bathroom," she lied.

"Oh." He paused awkwardly. "May I come in?"

"If you remove your hat." A meager power play.

He did it and stepped forward. "Look, Monica," he began on a softer note, but she had no wish to hear either feeble excuses or maudlin words of farewell. His powerful presence was heart-wrenching enough.

"Please," she interrupted, "I've really got tons to do. Say what you have to say and then let me get back to work."

Any softness that might have found its way into Michael's voice had now vanished. He drew himself up even straighter. "I've got to take care of something. I'll be out of town for a few days. I've arranged for a friend,

Steve Wright, to meet you after work and walk you home."

"That's absurd!" she exploded, her temper a product of thirty-six hours of hell. "It was bad enough when you came last night. But I won't have someone else making me all the more embarrassed."

"He's a cop—"

"So much the worse!" She watched as the muscles in his cheek tightened, wondering how he could look even sterner. But he did. And loving him as she did, it hurt. "I won't be escorted across the Common like a criminal."

"He'll be out of uniform."

"I don't care! Don't you understand that I don't want your help?" It wasn't entirely the truth but what she really wanted was his love, and that seemed dreams away.

Michael scowled, on the verge of an outburst of his own, when his eye caught the opened box of flowers. "Ahhh . . . she's got a suitor," he drawled tightly. "That's very lovely. I'm sorry I didn't think of it first. But, then"—he stiffened and went on more icily—"you didn't strike me as the type to be swayed by long-stemmed roses." Pausing only for a moment's glower, he replaced his hat. "Go back to work," he muttered scornfully, then turned his back and left.

When Monica could move, she shut the

door quietly and just as quietly broke down in tears. Soft sobs were muffled behind her hands as she struggled to understand how she had so sadly botched her relationship with Michael. As a woman who thought she controlled her destiny, she had proven to be a total failure.

What had happened to the man she loved? Where had he gone? Had he been swallowed up in that sea of navy blue she detested? Where were those warm embraces, those fiery kisses, and that intimately bantering give-and-take that had characterized their times together? Yes, they'd argued then. But anger had always melted before that greater fire. Had it gone out for good?

That night's show was uneventful, as was Wednesday's and Thursday's. After each show Monica suffered the silent indignity of being met by a surprisingly pleasant and frankly respectful Steve Wright and walked safely home across the Common. Once in her apartment, the only solace to be found was in reading. In dire need of a happy ending she purposely picked up *The Rainbow's End*. And so she waited for something to happen.

Still in the box in which they'd been delivered, the long-stemmed white roses had long since wilted in a back-alley trash can. Though he hadn't sent them, they could only

remind her of Michael. She had received no
further calls, either at home or on the air. For
that she was grateful. Unfortunately the
pickpocket hadn't totally been idle—he hit
twice during the course of the week, once on
Wednesday and again on the following day.
It was Thursday's robbery that she read
about in Friday morning's paper—right next
to a blurb on the aging but esteemed Commissioner of Police, who, it seemed, had
been admitted to the Massachusetts General
Hospital for coronary bypass surgery.

"Terrific," she grumbled on a sour note,
feeling in need of some sort of bypass herself. Much as she might hide beneath
makeup, her early-morning mirror couldn't
lie. She looked pale and wan, and felt every
bit as lifeless. Something was definitely going to have to give.

It did. Shortly after lunch the buzzer rang.
She'd been disciplining herself to read a
short murder mystery, one of a series written
by her segment B guest. It was more grue-
some than she personally liked, particularly
in light of the spooking-up she'd had in recent days. The doorbell was a momentary
savior—until her stomach filled with butter-
flies.

Too often in the past the doorbell had
brought heartache. If this was more of the

same, she couldn't face it. A quick look out the window down toward the street brought no answers. There was no cruiser—was she disappointed? There were neither a parcel truck nor any sign of another delivery. For an instant she toyed with the idea of not answering the door. She wasn't in the mood for visitors and anyone else would leave a message. Then the sound of the buzzer shot through her again. With a soft curse she responded.

"Yes?"

"Ms. Grant?"

"Yes."

"Delivery. Chocolates."

Chocolates? What kind of joke was this? Last time she'd been fanciful enough to imagine a present from Michael. This time she hoped she knew better. Last time the gift had been from "an ever-loyal fan." Would the same one be sending her candy?

"Leave them there," she demanded impulsively. "I'll get them on my way out."

"Fine," said the faceless voice, then was gone.

Monica stood waiting for several minutes, watching an overweight man dressed in some sort of uniform leave her building and disappear down the street. Was this the fan whom she'd turned away, or was he indeed a delivery man? Was someone else—perhaps even Sammy—trying to cheer her up? Poor Sammy. He couldn't have helped but see her sorry state this week.

Feeling decidedly sheepish she went downstairs, picked up the package, and returned to her apartment. Once locked back inside, she set it on the coffee table and removed its outer wrapping. Inside was a gaily decorated box. This too she opened, but more timidly. In fact, she *had* received a gift of chocolates, imported at that and filled with assorted liqueurs. But from whom? She reached hesitantly for the card that lay prominently atop the button-round sweets. Her hands were unsteady as she opened it, worse when she recognized the handwriting as the same that had been in the note with the roses.

Dear Monica, she read. *I'm still listening to the show, loving it when the sparks really fly. Enjoy this little treat. But be sure not to eat too many at once.* It was signed this time, *Your faithful follower.*

In a fit of temper Monica tore the card into a handful of tiny pieces, gathered them together in her lap, and dumped them into the kitchen wastebasket. But why was she so upset? Just because one of her listeners had taken her to heart? Or was it this breach of her privacy that she resented . . . or the eeriness of not knowing her follower's name? Or . . . was it simply that *Michael* hadn't sent her candy . . .

Then the front buzzer sounded again. "Oh, no!" she cried, wishing only to bury herself somewhere and be free from this nagging torment. "Go away," she whispered, but the sound came again and again beneath an impatient finger. "Leave me alone!"

She had no such luck. When the caller finally despaired of her answering, she returned on shaky legs to the living room, only to be jolted by a knocking on her door.

"Monica? Are you there?" His muffled voice penetrated the wood.

With instant recognition came fury. It was a moment of déjà-vu. With several swift steps she flung the door open. "Of course I'm here. But if I don't answer the buzzer, it means I don't want to be disturbed." She lowered her voice at the end only as she saw her landlady, a quiet elderly woman, with the master key in her hand.

"It's all right, ma'am," Michael said to her landlady. "Thank you for your help. I'll take it from here."

Monica felt her blood pound angrily through her veins as she waited for the woman to reach the first landing. Then she turned on Michael. "Take *what* from here?"

"Get inside," he commanded quietly, looking forbidding in uniform with his hat drawn low on his brow. Realizing that the privacy would benefit them both, she acquiesced. She also realized that she was overreacting terribly. The fact that her motive forces were love and its anguish was small solace. With a sigh she determined to be civil at least. The role of the outraged shrew was not one she admired.

She walked to her peacock chair and settled gracefully into it, leaving Michael to shut the door and stand or sit as he wished. He stood, cap in hand, fingers sliding along its headband and back. She recalled how he'd stroked her as smoothly in the night and felt a deep pain for what had been lost. It was as though they were back to that first Tuesday afternoon when a patrolman had escorted her home in the line of duty. All that they'd shared seemed gone.

If Monica's eyes had reflected faraway thoughts, Michael's had mirrored the sojourn. For an instant, in the collision of their glances, there was transparency. She saw pain and vulnerability and loneliness—until the curtain descended on Michael the man. This was Shaw the cop stopping by for some unknown reason.

"Are you all right, Monica?" he asked,

looking unusually tired and drawn himself.
Too much running around, she mused spite-
fully.

"Steve could have answered that question. You didn't have to stop specially to ask
it." She hated herself for the sound of her
voice, but she hurt so incredibly much.

"I wanted to stop. Things are going okay?"

"Yes." She sighed. "Did you finish what
you were up to?"

He gave a rueful smile. "For now."

She nodded, then frowned and feigned
concentration on one slender finger as it lay
amid the others in her lap. Not knowing
what to say, she felt totally awkward. Was
this really Monica the Mouth sitting so
silently? Salazar and his cronies would be
amazed. But, then, wasn't Michael his crony,
more or less? Shaking her head at the sadness of it all, she waited for him to make his
move. Had she been looking at him, she
would have seen him shake his head as well,
but in disdain rather than sadness. The chill
in his voice compensated for what she'd
missed.

"Whew, you women are amazing! Too independent for your own good and fickle as
hell!"

Her head shot up. "What?" This was the
pot calling the kettle black.

"Your ardent admirer again?" he jeered, eyes pinpointing the candy on the table.

Having momentarily forgotten with the trauma of Michael's arrival, Monica caught her breath. "Actually they're from a . . . a friend." She really didn't want to fight, and this seemed like one way to avoid it. If she told him the truth, he'd only pester her more. She already felt drained.

"Who?"

"That's none of your business," she replied quietly.

"*Who?*" His brown-eyed gaze transfixed her, harsh and demanding.

"A . . . a neighbor."

"Male?"

There was still a certain residue of pride. "As it happens . . . yes." She tipped up her chin with a little white lie. "I watered his plants for him while he was on vacation, and this was his way of saying thank you." It seemed as good a story as any, and she had watered plants for a neighbor . . . except that it had been a *she* and the vacation had been the winter before.

"Convenient."

"And what is *that* supposed to mean?" she asked. He actually sounded jealous, and she simply couldn't fathom that.

"Ach . . . nothing," he said with a grimace.

"Listen, Monica . . ." His tone changed then from angry to unsure, and he seemed almost self-conscious. ". . . I wondered if we could . . . if I could . . . see you this weekend . . ."

"What?" she whispered, incredulous that after brushing her off all week he'd ask her out now. Then with a moment's acuity she understood and saw a bright and vivid shade of red. "Damn you!" she seethed, rising and storming to the window for want of a better place to rage. When she turned to face Michael, she was shaking with fury. Her eyes had gone far beyond glittering; they fairly sparked fire.

"So last weekend wasn't enough for you? You're hungry for more? And here's good old Monica who 'comes to life in my arms?' I've read that line so many times I could gag!" she screamed, then slapped her palm to her forehead. "And I actually thought you were different. God, was I stupid! A woman to warm your bed, that's all you want. And don't give me that bull about wanting my 'company.' You certainly didn't need my company all week. You had your cops-and-robbers games to occupy you then!" In her anger she'd been heedless of the fact that Michael had rounded the sofa and was now approaching.

"You're getting hysterical," he said warningly. She was beyond warning.

"I am *not* getting hysterical! A typical male response when a woman finally states the truth!"

"You don't know what you're saying—" His voice was in taut control.

"I know *precisely* what I'm saying!" She'd never been as furious—or as hurt—in her life. "And this is beginning to sound like a bottom-of-the-barrel novel. Why don't you leave, Michael, and take your raging virility with you. Find a woman who's satisfied with a weekend's exploitation here or there. *I'm not!*"

Suddenly purged of her rage, Monica stopped, then gasped. The face before her was an iron mask, every bit as furious as she'd been herself. "So you wanted chivalry all along—roses and candy and all those other doting gestures? Well, maybe I'm just not as traditional as I thought I was!" His nostrils flared as he sought to control his temper. "But I'll tell you one thing I *am* old-fashioned about and that's fidelity. I'd give my woman as much free rein as she wanted as long as it stopped short of wagging her tail in front of other men. So go ahead, Monica. String along your Sir Galahad, and maybe he'll send you jewels next time. Of course, he's bound to want something in return. Will you tear off your clothes for him like you did for me?" At the far end of outrage Monica brought her hand swiftly around, but it was as swiftly intercepted and held in midair. "I wouldn't do that if I were you," he drawled, seeming suddenly more sure. "If you were to hit me, I'd surely have to avenge my virility by taking you right here on the floor. And I can promise I wouldn't be gentle."

She couldn't believe what was happening, couldn't think straight. The only thing she knew was that Michael couldn't possibly hurt her any more than he already had. The outright disdain he held for her was excruciating.

"Please leave," she whispered, refusing to let him see her in tears.

He released her wrist with deliberate slowness and bent to retrieve the cap he'd let drop to the chair. Then his eye caught the box of candy open on the table. Looking back at her once, he helped himself to a piece, popping it into his mouth and making an event of its consumption.

"Not bad," he said with insolence. "A mite tart . . ." His gaze said the rest as he brashly raked her trembling form. Then he eased the hat onto his head, lazily adjusted it, walked slowly to the door, and let himself out.

Monica found herself in a state of suspension, not knowing whether to yell first or cry. As it happened she did a little of each, pacing the floor of her apartment muttering a stream of derogatory phrases while tears poured down her cheeks.

"And that's *his* view of the modern woman, jumping from bed to bed with no scruples at all!" Chest heaving, she paused in the kitchen to pound a fist on the table. "Well, damn him! He can just find some little tramp in the Combat Zone. Serve him right if he catches a ghastly disease!" And she stormed back through to the living room. "Who does he think he is—walking in here expecting me to fall at his feet after the way he ignored me all week. He could have called! Even when he was away. It wouldn't have broken him to put a dime in the slot!" Pausing to rest against the back of the sofa when the throes of weeping shook her, she pressed her fingers to her eyes.

But with an easing of her sobs came a renewal of anger. "How *dare* he do that! That was all he wanted—a warm and responsive body. That's all men want anyway!" Teeth clenched, she whirled around. "And I was stupid. *Stupid!*" Spying the candy that sat so innocently in witness to her rage, she reached over to shove one in her mouth, then a second. " 'Don't eat too many at a time,' he writes—as if I'm an imbecile and can't take care of myself." Her voice lowered to a whisper of disgust. "They're *all* a bunch of scheming egotists. Manipulating. Self-centered. Aching to be put on that pedestal." She reached for a third candy out of pure spite, swallowed it without the slightest awareness of its taste, and charged into the bathroom as she ranted more quietly, "They'll get theirs . . ."

A long shower didn't help, other than repairing the ravages of her tears and leaving her squeaky clean from head to toe. She felt awful.

Letting her hair dry loose in the warmth of the afternoon air, she pulled on a fresh T-shirt and a pair of shorts, then padded barefoot to the balcony and sat on the chaise. She glared out over the city but saw absolutely nothing at all. Glancing sideways, she spotted *The Rainbow's End*, but the thought of reading it curdled her stomach. It would only serve to emphasize all that she didn't have . . . and she couldn't bear that.

She thought of the show tonight, and her stomach felt queasy. How could she possibly go on the air after what she'd just been through? She felt as though she couldn't move, let alone finish her preparations and host a stimulating three hours' worth of conversation. Though she'd never called in sick before, she knew that one of the other members of the staff could cover for her in an emergency. Should she call in sick now? She wasn't *really* sick aside from a nervous stomach. The illness was mainly in her mind.

That mind refused to be eased by rationalization. It did no good to tell herself that she was better without Michael, that her future was still secure, that she'd perhaps even find another love one day. She still ached for him.

Bounding up in frustration, she stalked toward the kitchen, where the book she'd been reading lay open on the table. She sat down and read a page, then reread it when she realized she hadn't absorbed a word. It was as dry the second time around. And the gnawing in her stomach was that much worse, sitting sternly at the table as she was.

Mystery in hand, she returned to the balcony, but the book met the same fate there. She couldn't concentrate. It was as simple and annoying as that. She swore in anger once more at the thought that a man might rule her life like this and cursed the day she'd been picked up from the sidewalk by the solicitous Michael Shaw.

At the mention of his name her stomach cramped and she doubled over in pain.

When the spasm passed, she lay back on the chaise and damned her own vulnerability. How could she have let herself fall in love with the man? She knew what he was. She'd been right all along. Thank goodness he'd be leaving in September.

Another cramp seized her, more severely this time and lingering. Knees bent up to her chest, she mopped a sheen of perspiration from her nose. Perhaps she should take something, she mused. But the pain gradually passed, and she relaxed back once more.

She needed a vacation. That was it. It had been too long since she'd been away for more than a night or two. Last Thanksgiving she'd gone home. She smiled. That had been nice. Perhaps she'd take off at the end of August and go north for a week. She'd always wanted to explore the Gaspé Peninsula. It might be fun to drive along leisurely. Then she frowned, recalling last weekend's leisurely drive. That had been heaven . . .

She jackknifed under the force of a third cramp and struggled to catch her breath. This was hell. What *was* the matter? She'd never been prone to psychosomatic illness before. As upset as she was about Michael, she simply couldn't believe her body would betray her this way. With shallow gasps she clutched at her stomach. Something was wrong. Was it something she'd eaten? Another spasm shook her, its pain overlapping that of its predecessor. In that instant Monica knew there was something *very* wrong.

The heat seemed suddenly oppressive, and forcing herself around, she stumbled back into the apartment. She barely made it to the sofa before another wave of cramping began. Whiteknuckled, she held herself, eyes shut, trying to find a cause for this attack. When she dared to look up, she spotted the box of candy.

The candy. Was it possible? She was in excellent health, and her lunch had consisted of the same yogurt and toast she'd been eating for years. *What other possibility was there?* Candy sent to her by an admirer. An admirer . . . a fan of hers. That was what the pickpocket had called himself . . . a fan of hers.

The pickpocket? Suddenly she saw things clearly, as she should have seen them days ago. The pickpocket! How could she have been so blind, so stubborn? *He* was the admirer who'd sent the flowers, then the candy. Could he have put something in the candies? The package had looked so pretty, the contents had appeared untouched. He was a man who had already been charged

with manslaughter. What more did he have
to lose?

The pain seemed constant now, aggra-
vated with each cramp and steadily getting
worse. Poison? *Poison?* Whatever . . . it
didn't seem to matter. She needed help.

Then she cried aloud as a thought hit her,
simultaneously with a hard shooting pain.
Michael! Michael had eaten the candy too! If
anything ever happened to him . . .

It was sheer force of determination that
got her to the telephone, sheer desperation
that dredged up the police emergency number and punched in that 911, sheer
willpower that produced a voice when her
breath was stolen by one stabbing pain after
the other.

"Emergency. Officer Strom."

"Get Michael Shaw," she gasped. "District One. He's a policeman. Call him on your
radio." She paused, huddled against the
wall, panting away dizziness. "Tell him it's
Monica. Monica Winslow. *Winslow*" They
couldn't ignore her now. "Poison. The candy
was poisoned." Tears flowed slowly from her
pain-shrouded eyes. "He has to get to a hospital. He'll be sick. Tell him. *Tell him!*"

"Where are you calling from?" The voice
at the other end seemed instinctively aware
of her own problem.

"West Cedar," she rasped. "One forty-five. I . . . need help." It seemed to be a losing battle against the pain. She whimpered weakly. "Get help here. But . . . get Michael first. Michael Shaw."

"Help is on the way, Miss Winslow. But listen to me." It took every bit of her strength to hold the receiver, but she did. "I want you to go to the front door and leave it ajar. Can you walk?"

"I think so," she whispered brokenly.

"Then go to the door now. I'll have a cruiser there in a matter of minutes. Okay?"

She barely had a chance to nod her head before she buckled in pain. Leaving the receiver dangling from its hook, she half-staggered, half-scrambled to the door, knowing, as did the officer, that if she didn't open it now before she was even more incapacitated precious seconds would be wasted when help did arrive.

Crying in fear, she slid down against the doorjamb to the floor. Michael had to be all right. Had to be all right. If he could get to the hospital in time . . . get an antidote. But what kind of poison was it? How would the doctors ever know what to give him? If anything happened to him she'd never forgive herself. Just as well she'd eaten three candies to his one . . .

What a fool she'd been. If only she could tell him that. She should have listened to him when he warned her about this pickpocket. She'd been too smug, too arrogant, to believe herself in danger. But Michael had known. He'd known.

Curled tightly in a ball, she pressed her forehead to her knees. Weeping, crying out in pain, moaning in mental torment—it was all the same now. She'd never even told him she loved him . . .

It seemed forever that she waited, torn apart even more with every agonizing second. Her insides were a squirming bundle of raw nerves riddled with pain. Surely unconsciousness was preferable to this. But Michael's face dominated her mind-screen. She couldn't shut her eyes to it. He had to be all right . . .

"Monica?" A strange voice broke into her delirium, a strange touch pulled her hair from her face. Both were uncommonly gentle.

"Michael?" she cried through a thick haze of pain.

"It's all right," the voice said soothingly. "He's on his way to the hospital. He'll meet us there. I'm John, my partner's Tony. I'm going to carry you downstairs now, okay?"

Monica forced her eyes open to focus on the uniformed patrolman crouched by her side. She'd never seen anything as beautiful as that badge on his breast pocket. It was taken from view though, when he slipped his arms carefully around her and lifted her against him.

"Michael? Is Michael all right?" she gasped through the agony of being moved.

"He'll be fine," returned the reassuring voice. "You'll see him in a couple of minutes." Then he directed himself to his partner. "Got it, Tony?"

The other voice was behind them. "The whole box. On the coffee table, like Mike said."

"Okay. Let's go."

Held tightly by this stranger she'd never seen before, Monica was carried down the stairs to the waiting cruiser. The breadth of his chest absorbed her agonized moans. "It's all right, Monica," he said soothingly. "Everything's going to be all right."

She barely remembered the three minutes' drive to Mass. General, mercifully just on the other side of Beacon Hill. She knew that she was held the whole way, that her guardian had her out of the car before it had even come to a dead stop, that he ran with her toward the emergency room entrance before transferring her to a pair of more familiar arms.

"Michael?" she croaked, fearful she was hallucinating. "Michael?"

"I'm here," he whispered on the run, helplessly watching her clutch her stomach as they entered a room filled with waiting medical personnel. He brushed his lips against her damp brow and held her for a protective instant before carefully setting her down on the gurney. Others had already begun to close in on her, but she clutched his hand convulsively.

"You're all right?" she gasped. She couldn't seem to see any more clearly than she could think. Only this one thought was concrete. Michael had to be all right.

"I'm fine . . . and you will be too." He held her hand tighter as she tried to ride with the oncoming wave of pain, but other hands held her too and Michael was gently ushered aside.

Ten

When the commotion finally died down and she was able to grasp reality once more, Monica found herself in a quiet, dimly lit room, lying in a bed that seemed inordinately uncomfortable. She ached all over and felt very, very tired.

Michael was sitting in a chair not far from the bed, his elbows propped up on his knees, his hands tightly clenched. At the first sign of her stirring he moved closer. "How do you feel?" he asked softly.

Her voice was not much more than a motion of her lips. "Awful." But he was all right. He was! She saw his face clearly, and its gentleness compensated for her lingering physical discomfort. The intense pain was gone now, but she was weak and sore. She felt his fingers smooth her hair from her cheek and surrendered to their pacifying touch. With a sigh she drifted off to sleep again.

When she awoke, he was there still, looking tired, but he came to life when she turned her head on the pillow. Moving closer, he put her hand to his lips. Then he held it between his palms and looked at her soulfully.

"Any better?"

She moved experimentally, then paused, spent. "Why do I feel so raw?" she whispered, unable to find the strength to produce sound.

"You've been through an ordeal. What you feel now is a normal reaction to having one's stomach pumped."

Moaning, she closed her eyes again. It was too painful to think back, to remember the bits and snatches of the past few hours. The only thing that mattered was that Michael was well. All else would have to wait.

But only until she woke up again. Then a deluge of questions flooded her mind. It was morning, as announced by the pale light seeping through the window blinds. She felt much more rested, though still achy. Michael sat slumped in his seat, waking up with a jolt when she reached for a glass of water from the bedstand. He poured it for her instantly.

"Here. Drink slowly." He held the glass while she sipped from a straw.

"My throat hurts. It's so dry," she croaked, sounding thoroughly hoarse.

"It'll hurt for a day or two. Do you feel better otherwise?"

She nodded, unable to take her eyes from his face. He looked terrible, tense and tired. But he was functioning on his own—which was more than she could say for herself. "You didn't get sick too?" she asked on a note of incredulity.

Placing the glass back on the stand, he sat down on the bed by her hip. His hand closed over hers. "He only injected *some* of the candies with the stuff. It was like a game of Russian roulette. I lucked out. You . . . didn't."

"What was it?" Her voice was getting weaker.

"Just a little strychnine."

"*Strychnine?*"

"Shhh. Try to rest."

"Strychnine . . . as in *rat* poison?"

"The same. But it's gone. No need to worry. Your stomach's as clean as a whistle."

His humor was lost on her, her mind having moved on to other things. "Michael, I—"

"Shhhh." He put a finger against her lips. But she felt herself getting drowsy again and knew she had something to tell him that simply couldn't wait.

"I love you, Michael," she whispered. "I just wanted you to know that." Her lids were heavy, and she let them fall. Somehow she didn't care what his reaction was now that she'd said what she had to say. The words were still on her lips and Michael was still sitting on the bed when she opened her eyes once more. It was an hour later and that much brighter. He studied the slow return of color to her cheeks and evidenced his satisfaction by relaxing his features. His eyes were warm, casting off their own fatigue to soothe her.

"Hi," he whispered with a gentle smile.

"I love you. I was so afraid something might have happened to you." She rushed the words out, desperate for expression. "I do love you." Her voice had a husky tone that would have been seductive in any other situation.

Leaning forward, Michael put his lips lightly to hers. "Don't talk now. Save your voice."

Feeling the urgency of confession, she promptly ignored him. "I've been stubborn. It was foolish of me. You were right about so many things."

Before her eyes Michael tensed. "There
are things I've got to tell you," he said
solemnly. "I've been foolish myself. There
are things you should have known from the
start."

Monica felt the strain of her heartbeat
against inner muscles that were still weak.
Her gaze must have reflected the pain, for
Michael took her into his arms and hugged
her fiercely. That was the moment the doctor
chose to appear.

Fortunately little was asked of Monica
save nodding or shaking her head during his
brief examination. Michael did most of the
talking, and she tuned out, closing her eyes,
turning her head to the side. *Things you
should have known from the start.* What
kind of things? She'd known all along that
there was a mystery about him, that certain
things didn't jive with the life of the policeman. She'd heard the story about his background, his decision to wear the blue. But
Wisconsin . . . and Boston . . . and that transfer program she'd never heard of. Or, she
frowned, still with her eyes closed tight,
what if he'd lied and there was a woman in
his life? What if she *was* nothing more than
handy summer entertainment?

A pair of gentle lips touched the furrows
on her brow and her eyes flew open. "Would

you like to get dressed and leave now . . . or wait until after breakfast?" he asked softly, indulgently.

"Leave?" It took a minute for her to comprehend. Even then there were more pressing matters. "What things, Michael? Tell me."

He took her arms and lifted her to a sitting position. "Let's get out of here. We can talk later."

"No . . . now!" she burst out in a raspy exclamation. "What things should I have known from the start?"

Michael shook his head then raked his fingers through his hair. "You're right. You are stubborn."

"What things?" As she stared at him she saw a look of defeat that she'd never seen before. "You're *not* divorced?"

"Of course I'm divorced. I was divorced years and years ago."

"Then there's a woman waiting back in Wisconsin?"

Puzzled, he shook his head. "No."

Her eyes widened, anguish-filled. "Another woman *here?*"

"No!"

"Then what is it?"

With a deep sigh he shifted uncomfortably and bowed his head. "It wasn't really a transfer program that brought me here, Monica."

"Here it comes," she whispered, but he went on, barely hearing.

"I told you that I'd entered the Wisconsin department in an upper-level capacity." She held her breath when he raised his eyes to meet hers. "I've spent the past three years as the chief of police there. As of . . . next week, it looks like . . . I'll be the police commissioner here."

"And . . . ?"

He eyed her strangely. "That's all."

"That's your deep, dark secret?" She felt a surge of warm relief.

"It's bad enough! I've deceived you . . . even in spite of the intimacy of our relationship."

"Oh, Michael," she sighed. "I thought there was something *wrong!*" She reached out to clasp his hand. "That's a wonderful secret! I'm so proud of you."

"*Proud* of me . . . after hiding the truth from you all these weeks?"

"Yes. Proud of you." She smiled with amazing buoyancy, even as a sense of anticipation crept up. There was only one thing she wanted to hear now. She wouldn't have dared hope for it twenty-four hours ago. But he'd been here at the hospital waiting for her, sitting with her through the night, now confessing his self-disgust at having been less than truthful with her. Only one thing . . . She waited on that thread of hope.

"But I've blown your trust!" he exclaimed in dismay.

"You haven't blown my anything," she replied softly, savoring the role of comforter for a change. "You've been right all along about so many other things. I'm sure you had your reasons." She held her breath and waited.

"They weren't terribly noble," he offered apologetically.

"You must have felt they were valid." Well . . . ?

"At the time . . . yes." He paused, and she held his gaze expectantly. Still he denied her those three simple words. "I came to Boston in June with total anonymity. What I wanted to do was to get to know both the city and the department from the ground floor. My pending appointment was a well kept secret between the mayor, one or two people in his office, and the present police commissioner. When I first met you I was strictly under cover. When I found out who you were and got an earful of that reputation of yours, I was doubly frightened. My cover could have been blown so easily if you'd let something slip on your show. You'd already made it clear how you felt toward the police."

"I had, hadn't I?" She recalled that initial sparring and smirked.

But his gaze mirrored the anguish he must have felt then. "I found you fascinating from the start. Challenging. And I thought I saw similar needs in you that made you . . . different from . . . my ex-wife."

He took a breath. "But I tried to stay away from you."

"I remember," she whispered, beginning to wonder if her hope was unfounded. He seemed to be stalling for time—or were his priorities simply ordered differently? Did he love her . . . or didn't he?

"Things got more complicated after that," he went on intently. "When I found myself so strongly attracted to you, I think I used this uniform"—he glanced down at his navy blues—"as a shield. I'd been burned once by an independent woman. The cover I'd adopted seemed one way to keep some kind of distance between us."

"It didn't work," she mused aloud.

"No." His chuckle was a knowing one and a sign of reemerging humor. He kissed her gently and let his lips linger for a quiet moment.

Monica lay still, beginning to grow more

impatient. But this was his show, and she was determined to let him run it at his own pace. She thought she'd die when he picked up the narrative right where he'd left off.

"As a matter of fact it backfired! I couldn't keep my distance, but the closer I got, the worse it was to uphold the deception. I wanted you to know the truth, but I wasn't sure I could trust you. Then when I knew for certain that I could, I felt so damned guilty about having held back the truth that I didn't have the guts to spill it all." His voice grew less steady. "I was frightened, Monica," he explained, stroking her cheek with a whispered caress. "I was frightened you'd hate me for it."

"How could I ever hate you? I *love* you," she breathed, then held her breath. Okay, Shaw. Let's *hear* it already.

"Do you?" he asked, seeming truly doubtful. "You've practically spat at me every time I've seen you."

"Not last weekend," she chided hoarsely. "Didn't that tell you anything?" Come on . . . come on . . .

He arched a brow suggestively. "That could have been pure physical passion. We were good together, weren't we?"

"Good? What that was was *spectacular!*"

"Shhhhh. You sound like a gravel-voiced analyst."

Then don't keep me waiting like this! "But I'm right," she went on in a quieter, gritty voice. "And physical passion accounted for only part of my response. You should know that. On second thought, no you shouldn't. You're a man! What does a man know about love?" It was the perfect opening. If anything could spur him on, this would.

It didn't. "There you go with your feminist propaganda again. Just when I thought you'd finally come to your senses." She rose to the bait, narrowing her eyes in frustration.

"You are an arrogant beast. And I have no idea why I love you the way I do."

"Maybe because you've begun to accept the presence of that old-fashioned girl deep within you." He drew the back of his fingers down the front of her gown, between her breasts to her navel.

"Michael!"

"Yes?"

"What are you doing?" Frustration was building on several fronts now.

"Me? Nothing."

"That isn't 'nothing.' And it isn't fair. I'm sick." And getting tired of waiting.

"You're not sick. You can leave right now with me. I'll fix you some breakfast back at my place."

So he wanted her in his den with no promises made? Of all the presumptuous . . . "You said you didn't know how to cook."

"No problem. You're on a very limited diet anyway. Doctor's orders for the weekend. Tea and toast and all kinds of bland goodies. Right up my alley."

"I'm not going to your place."

"Why not?"

"I can go to mine—" Then she caught her breath as the thought of her own adored apartment brought a wave of terror. "I can't! He knows! He sent those things, you know— the flowers *and* the candy."

"I know," Michael replied smugly.

His calm evoked her instant suspicion. "What else do you know?" she asked, despairing of his true confession for the moment.

"He's in custody."

"What?"

"Shhh. Your voice."

"Tell me, Michael!"

"He called the show last night to find out what was wrong with you."

"The show!" she exclaimed huskily. "I completely forgot about the show!"

"Sammy covered, with Ben Thorpe in the wings. When your friend called in—"

"He's not my friend!"

"Shhh. Monica . . . keep it down."

She searched the ceiling for the patience that seemed to have flown. "Okay," she whispered. "Go on."

Michael took pleasure in drawing out the suspense. "When the pickpocket called in, he was very upset, close to panic that you were sick. He had only intended to scare you and to feel a little power while he was at it. He said"—Michael eyed her in an accusatory way—"that he warned you against eating too many."

So he had. "I only ate three."

"Three too many . . . but that's beside the point. Ben was able to keep him on the line long enough for—"

"—the call to be traced." She nodded as though it were the only logical thing . . . which it was. "Oh, Michael . . . I was stupid! Bullheaded!"

"Um-hmm."

She sank back onto the bed, feeling tired and discouraged. "And I was so wrong about your friends. Steve Wright was the nicest guy and those two—John and Tony—who came for me yesterday were wonderful. They were there when I needed them."

"Um-hmm."

Turning her head to the side, she closed her eyes. Something was still missing, but she didn't have the strength to ask. She couldn't force Michael to love her, and all the hoping in the world wouldn't make it happen if it hadn't already. Last night she had panicked at the thought of losing him to a madman's prank. Only now did she realize that she'd never really had him at all.

The burning sensation behind her eyes had nothing to do with the physical ordeal she'd endured, nor did the tightness that seized her throat. One tear, then another slowly slipped from the edge of her lids, and she bit her lip to keep her chin steady.

Then she felt him leaning forward, felt the warmth of his breath by her ear. "Have I told you how much I love you?" he asked softly. A whole new world of tenderness flowed in the velvet of his voice.

Monica's eyes flew open, filled with tears of hope. "No, you haven't!" she cried in a scratchy voice. "You've told me everything else—everything that's secondary! But the one thing I've been lying here just waiting to hear—you didn't bother!"

Michael slid his fingers into her hair and brushed at her tears with the gentle pad of his thumb. "I'm bothering now," he reached her soul. "I love you, Monica."

"Oh . . . Michael . . ." The tears flowed faster, and she felt like a child. But her smile was all woman, as were the arms that reached up to him. When he took her to him, she knew she'd found her man.

It was later that day, as they lay molded together in the hammock on Michael's balcony, that they talked of the future. "You won't mind being married to a cop?"

"I wouldn't exactly call you a cop." She twisted her fingers in the soft hair on his chest.

"A cop once removed then. It's a matter of semantics."

"Michael," she took a breath, "I'd marry you if you were a sanitation engineer—I'm that much in love with you."

"You're sure?" he asked, needing the reassurance.

"Very. . . . You know"—she tipped back her head to look at him—"I was with a fellow back in Phoenix. We were together for nearly two years. We just . . . drifted painlessly apart. That was a long time ago, but I've often wondered whether I'd be able to trust love again. I mean, we thought we were in love, did all the right things, said all the right words. Yet . . . it was gone without so much as a tear. Would I be able to commit myself to marriage . . . knowing that love was . . . ephemeral?"

"Will you?"

"Yes." She smiled, without any doubt. "*This* is love, and it's different from anything I've ever known before. I've been in agony all week, knowing that I loved you but fearing that you didn't feel the same. I knew then that I'd love you forever—even if it meant having to learn to live with that pain. And then I got sick and thought you'd be sick too." She shuddered, then went on in a plaintive whisper. "I don't think I could go on . . . if anything ever happened to you."

"You'd go on," he countered softly. "You're one strong lady. That's part of what I love about you. And if you have any intention of going soft on me . . . don't!"

Monica laughed. "I don't think I could change *that* much. As it is I've come a long way."

"Not really, love. You've just begun to let loose that very basic need for love and trust and commitment. For someone to lean on sometimes or be strong for when they need to lean on you. A need we all have, love." The silence of the night air caressed them for a moment. When Michael spoke again, it was in a hushed tone. "It was that very first day that I suspected a warm streak in you. When I took you back to your apartment and saw those figures on your mantel . . . you know . . . the ones your friend in Vermont carved?" She nodded. "I haven't been able to forget the one of a mother and her child. Will you nurse our child one day?"

Waiting for her throat muscles to relax, she rubbed her cheek against his warm, welcoming chest. "I wouldn't have it any other way," she whispered, eyes glowing to herald a dream come true.

"And I wouldn't have you any other way. Do you know that?" Shifting, he lowered his lips to hers and kissed her in a most convincing way. "I'm proud of you, too, Monica. You've built an exciting career for yourself." His voice lowered seductively. "Now if we can just get your hours shifted to the daytime, we'll be able to have our nights to ourselves."

Monica found that idea to be divine. "I think Sammy would put in a good word to the higher-ups. I kinda like you all to myself right at sunset time like this. Must be that romantic gene in me."

"That makes two of us," he murmured against her lips, instants before he gave her a long, loving kiss. Then they sighed against one another and lapsed into an intimate silence. Words were superfluous to the harmony that flowed warm in the summer's breeze. She'd never felt as content, as whole, and Michael shared the sentiment exactly. It was only when the sun's reflection turned orange over the harbor that he returned to a matter of business.

"There's going to be a press conference called for Monday morning to announce the commissioner's early retirement."

"How's he doing?"

"When I called a little while ago, he was doing well. But the recovery will be a slow one, and he's more than happy to turn over the department now. That's where I was this week, by the way—down at the Cape talking shop with him. He wouldn't rest easy until he'd unburdened himself of his thoughts about the department and its future. With his health being so poor, he was going to announce his retirement next month anyway. We're just pushing it up a bit." He paused, seeming unsure. "About this press conference . . ."

"Yes?"

"I'd like you by my side. Would you . . . would you come?"

"Did you *doubt* it?"

"Well, I know how you feel about the department."

"The department be damned. It's *you* I love! I wouldn't dream of being anywhere else on Monday morning!"

With a groan Michael enveloped her in a huge bear hug. "How did I ever deserve you?" he rasped, his voice huskier at that point than hers.

"You're a full-blooded American hero . . . and I'm an incurable romantic. How else could this have ended?"

He gave her a punishing squeeze. "You weren't so sure about that this morning."

"That was because my mind was addled. It's one thing to read about it and quite another to live it. Had I been able to sit back calmly and analyze what had happened, I would have recognized the typical eleventh-hour misunderstanding—you know, when I was hurt because you'd been so distant, and I reacted angrily, and then you thought I'd taken up with someone else, so you accused me of being a tramp, and then I got all the more furious—"

"Monica!"

"Yes, Michael?" She loved the scent of him, could breathe in his tang from one hour to the next.

"That's enough!"

"But I haven't mentioned the other problem." And his skin—so firmly textured. She loved to touch him—all over.

"What other problem?"

"This morning. You were supposed to tell me you loved me the very minute I woke up! You weren't supposed to let hours drag by before leisurely letting me know," she scolded playfully.

"*That*, my dear woman, is the difference between fact and fiction. It's my prerogative to surprise you once in a while."

Monica grinned and cuddled more sweetly against this man who thrilled her beyond imagination. *The Rainbow's End* had nothing on her. She and Michael had it all.

Now in hardcover from William Morrow,

an unforgettable story of love, loss,

and rebuilding a life,

Barbara Delinsky's

A WOMAN BETRAYED

The silence was deafening. Laura Frye sat in a corner of the leather sofa in the den, hugged her knees, and listened to it, minute after minute after minute. The wheeze of the heat through the vents couldn't pierce it. Nor could the slap of the rain on the windows, or the rhythmic tick of the small ship's clock on the shelf behind the desk.

It was five in the morning, and her husband still wasn't home. He hadn't called. He hadn't sent a message. His toothbrush was in the bathroom along with his razor, his after-shave, and the sterling comb and brush set Laura had given him for their twentieth anniversary the summer before. The contents of his closet were intact, right down to the small duffel he took with him to the sports club every Monday, Wednesday, and Friday. If he had slept somewhere else, he was totally ill equipped, which wasn't like Jeffrey at all, Laura knew. He was a precise man, a creature of habit. He never traveled, not for so much as a single night, without fresh underwear, a clean shirt, and a bar of deodorant soap.

More than that, he never went anywhere without telling Laura, and that was what frightened her most. She had no idea where he was or what had happened.

Not that she hadn't imagined. Laura wasn't usually prone to wild wanderings of the mind, but ten hours of waiting had taken its toll. She imagined that he'd had a stroke and lay unconscious across his desk in the deserted offices of Farro and Frye. She imagined that he'd been in an accident on the way home, that the car and everything in it had been burned beyond recognition or, alternately, that he had hit the windshield, climbed out, and begun wandering through the cold December rain not knowing who or where he was. She had gone so far as to imagine that he'd stopped for gas and had been taken hostage by a junkie holding up the nearby 7-Eleven.

More rational explanations for his absence had worn thin as night had waned. By no stretch of the imagination could she envision him holed up with a client at five in the morning. Maybe in April, with a new client whose tax records were in chaos but not the first week in December. And not without telling her. He always called if he was going to be late. Always.

Last night, they had been expected at an opening at the museum. Cherries had catered the affair. Though one of Laura's crews had handled the evening, she had spent the afternoon in Cherries' kitchen stuffing mushrooms, skewering smoked turkey and cherries, and cleaving baby lamb chops apart. She had wanted not only the food but the tables, the trays, and the bar to be perfect, which was why she had followed the truck to the museum to oversee the setting up.

Everything had been flawless. She had come home to change and get Jeff. But Jeff hadn't shown up.

Hugging her knees tighter in an attempt to fill the emptiness inside her, she stared at the phone. It had rung twice during the night. The first call had been from Elise, who was at the museum with her husband and wondered why Laura and Jeff weren't there. The second call had been from Donny for Debra, part of their nightly ritual. Sixteen-year-old sweethearts did that, Laura knew, just as surely as she knew that forty-something husbands who always called their wives if they were going to be late wouldn't not call unless something was wrong. So she had made several searching calls herself, but to no avail. The only thing she had learned was that the phone worked fine.

She willed it to ring now, willed Jeff to call and say he had had a late meeting with a client and had nearly fallen asleep at the wheel on the way home, so he'd pulled over to the side of the road to sleep off his fatigue. Of course, that wouldn't explain why the police hadn't spotted his car. Hampshire County wasn't so remote as to be without regular patrols or so seasoned as to take a shiny new Porsche for granted, particularly if that Porsche belonged to one half of a prominent Northampton couple.

The Frye name made the papers often, Jeff's with regard to the tax seminars he gave,

Laura's with regard to Cherries. The local press was a tough one, seeming to resist anything upscale, which the restaurant definitely was, but Laura fed enough luminaries on a regular basis to earn frequent mentions. *State Senator DiMento and his entourage were seen debating ways to trim fat from the budget over steamed vegetables and salads at Cherries this week*, wrote Duggan O'Neil of the *Hampshire County Sun*. Duggan O'Neil could cut people to shreds, and he had done his share of cutting where Laura was concerned, but publicity was publicity, Jeff said. Name recognition was important.

Indeed, the police officer with whom Laura had talked earlier on the phone had known just who she was. He even remembered Jeff's car as the one often parked outside the restaurant. But nothing in his records suggested that anyone in the department had seen or heard of the black Porsche that night.

"Tell you what, Miz Frye," he had told her. "Since it's you, I'll make a few calls. Throw in a piece of cherry cheesecake, and I'll even call the state police." But his calls had turned up nothing, and, to her dismay, he had refused to let her file a missing persons report. "Not until he's been gone twenty-four hours."

"But awful things can happen in twenty-four hours!"

"Good things, too, like lost husbands coming home."

Lost husbands coming home. She resented those words with a passion. They suggested she was inept as a wife, inept as a woman, that Jeff had been bored and gone looking for fun and would wander back home when the fun was over. Maybe the cop lived that way, but not Jeff and Laura Frye. They had been together for twenty good years. They loved each other.

So where was he? The question gnawed at her. She imagined him slain by a hitchhiker, accosted by Satanists, sucked up, Porsche and all, by an alien starship. The possibilities were endless, each one more bizarre than the next. Bizarre things did happen, she knew, but to other people. Not to her. And not to Jeff. He was the most steadfast, the most predictable, the most uncorruptible man she'd ever known, which was why his absence made no sense at all.

Unfolding her legs, she rose from the sofa and padded barefoot through the dark living room to the front window. Drawing back the sheers that hung beneath full-length silk swags, she looked out. The wind was up, ruffling the branches of the pines, driving the rain against the flagstone walk and the tall lamp at its head.

At least it wasn't snowing. She remembered times, early in her marriage, when she had been home with the children during storms, waiting for Jeff to return from work. He had been a new CPA then, a struggling one, and they had lived in a rented duplex. Laura used to stand at the window, playing games with the children, drawing pictures on the glass in the fog their breath made. Like clockwork, Jeff had always come through the snow, barely giving her time to worry.

He worked in a new building in the center of town now, and they weren't living in the duplex, or even in that first weathered Victorian, but in a gracious brick Tudor on a tree-lined street, less than a ten-minute drive from his office. It was a fast drive, an easy drive. But for some unknown and frightening reason he hadn't made it.

"Mom?"

Laura whirled around at the sudden sound

to find Debra beneath the living room arch. Her eyes were sleepy, her dark hair disheveled. She wore a nightshirt with UMASS COED NAKED LACROSSE splashed on the front over breasts that had taken a turn for the buxom in the past year.

Aware of her racing heart, Laura tried to smile. "Hi, Deb."

Debra sounded cross. "It's barely five. That's still the middle of the night, Mom. Why are you up?"

Unsure of what to say, just as she'd been unsure the night before when Debra had come home and Jeff hadn't been there, Laura threw back a gentle, "Why are you?"

"Because I woke up and remembered last night and started to worry. I mean, Dad's never late like that. I had a dream something awful happened, so I was going to check the garage and make sure the Porsche was—" Her voice stopped short. Her eyes probed Laura's in the dark. "It's there, isn't it?"

Laura shook her head.

"Where is he?"

She shrugged.

"Are you sure he didn't call and tell you something, and then you forgot? You're so busy, sometimes things slip your mind. O maybe he left a message on the machine, but it got erased. Maybe he spent the night at Nana Lydia's."

Laura had considered that possibility, which was why she had driven past her mother-in-law's house when she had gone out looking for Jeff. In theory, Lydia might have taken ill and called her son, though in all likelihood she would have called Laura first. Laura was her primary caretaker. She was the one who stocked the house with food, took her to the doctor, arranged for the cleaning girl or the exterminator or the plumber.

"He's not there. I checked."

"How about the office?"

"I went there too." To the dismay of the guard, who had looked far more sleepy than Debra, she had insisted on checking the garage for the Porsche, but Jeff's space—the entire garage under his building—had been empty.

"Is he with David?"

"No. I called." David Farro was Jeff's partner, but he hadn't known of any late meetings Jeff might have had. Nor had Jeff's secretary, who had left at five with Jeff still in his office.

"Maybe with a client?"

"Maybe."

"But you were supposed to go to the museum. Wouldn't he have called if he couldn't make it?"

"I would have thought so."

"Maybe something's wrong with the phone."

"No."

"Maybe he had car trouble."

But he would have called, Laura knew. Or had someone call for him. Or the police would have seen him and called.

"So where is he?" Debra cried.

Laura was terrified by her own helplessness. "I don't know!"

"He has to be *somewhere*!"

She wrapped her arms around her middle. "Do you have any suggestions?"

"Me?" Debra shot back. "What do I know? You're the adult around here. Besides, you're his wife. You're the one who knows him inside and out. You're supposed to know where he is." Turning back to the window, Laura drew the sheer aside and looked out again.

"Mom?"

"I don't know where he is, babe."

"Great. That's just great."

"No, it's not," Laura acknowledged, nervously scanning the street, "but there isn't an awful lot I can do right now. He'll show up, and I'm sure he'll have a perfectly good explanation for where he's been and why he hasn't called."

"If *I* ever stayed out all night without calling, you'd kill me."

"I may well kill your father," Laura said in a moment's burst of anger. Given what she'd been through, Jeff's explanation was going to have to be inspired if he hoped to be spared her fury. Then the fury died and fear returned. The possibilities flashed through her mind, one worse than the next. "He'll be home," she insisted, as much for her own sake as for Debra's.

"When?"

"Soon."

"How do you know?"

"I just know."

"What if he's sick, or hurt, or dying somewhere? What if he needs our help, but we're just standing here in a nice warm dry house waiting for him to show up? What if we're losing all this time when we should be out looking for him?"

Debra's questions weren't new. Laura had hit on all of them, more than once. Now she reasoned, "I looked for him last night. I drove around half the city and didn't see the Porsche.

I called the police, and they hadn't seen it either. If there was an accident, the police would call me."

"So you're just going to stand here looking out the window? Aren't you *upset?*"

Debra was a sixteen-year-old asking a frightened sixteen-year-old's questions. Laura was a frightened thirty-eight-year-old with no answers, which made her frustration all the greater. Keeping her voice as steady as possible, given the tremulous feeling she had inside, she turned to Debra and said, "Yes, I'm upset. Believe me, I'm upset. I've been upset since seven o'clock last night, when your father was an hour late."

"He never does this, Mom, *never.*"

"I know that, Debra. I went to his office. I drove around looking for his car. I called his partner, his secretary, and the police, but they won't do anything until he's been gone a day, and he hasn't been gone half that. What would you have me do? Walk the streets in the rain, calling his name?"

Debra's glare cut through the darkness. "You don't have to be sarcastic."

With a sigh, Laura crossed the floor and caught her daughter's hand. "I'm not being sarcastic. But I'm worried, and your criticism doesn't help."

"I didn't criticize."

"You did." Debra said what was on her mind and always had. Disapproval coming from a little squirt of a child hadn't been so bad. Disapproval coming from someone who was Laura's own five-six and weighed the same one-fifteen, who regularly borrowed Laura's clothes, makeup, and perfume, who drove a car, professed to know how to French-kiss, and was physically capable of having a child of her own was something else. "You think I should be doing more than I am," Laura argued, "but I'm hamstrung, don't you see? I don't know if anything's really wrong. There could be a logical reason for your father's absence. I don't want to blow things out of proportion before I have good cause."

"Twelve hours isn't good cause?" Debra cried and whirled around to leave, only to be held back by Laura's grip.

"Eleven hours," she said with quiet control. "And, yes, it's good cause, babe. But I can't do anything right now but wait. I can't do anything else." The silence that followed was heavy with an unspoken plea for understanding.

Debra lowered her chin. Her hair fell forward, shielding her from Laura's gaze. "What about me? What am I supposed to do?"

Scooping the hair back from Debra's face, Laura tucked it behind an ear. For an instant she caught a glimpse of her daughter's worry, but it was gone by the time Debra raised her head. In its place was defiance. Taking that as part and parcel of the spunk that made Debra special, Laura said, "What you're supposed to do is go back to bed. It's too early to be up."

"Sure. Great idea. Like I'd really be able to sleep." She shot a glance at Laura's sweater and jeans. "Like you really slept yourself." She turned her head a fraction and gave a twitch of her nose. "You've been cooking, haven't you? What's that smell?"

"Borscht."

"Oh, gross."

"It's not so bad." Jeff loved it with sour cream on top. Maybe, deep inside, Laura had been hoping the smell would lure him home.

"I can't believe you were cooking."

"I always cook."

"At work. Not at home. Most of the time you stick us with Chunky Chicken Soup, Frozen French Bread Pizza, or Microwave Meatballs and Spaghetti. You must feel guilty that Dad's missing."

Laura ignored the suggestion, which could have come straight from her own mother's analytical mouth. "He isn't missing, just late."

"So you cooked all night."

"Not all night. Just part of it." In addition to the borscht, she'd done a coq au vin she would probably freeze, since no one planned to be home for dinner for the next two nights. She had also baked a Black Forest cake and two batches of pillow cookies, one of which she would send to Scott.

"Did you sleep at all?" Debra asked.

"A little."

"Aren't you tired?"

"Nah. I'm fine." She was too anxious to sleep, which was why she had cooked. Normally, cooking relaxed her. It hadn't done that last night, but at least it had kept her hands busy.

"Well, I'm fine too," Debra declared. "I'll shower and dress and sit down here with you."

Laura knew what was coming. Debra was social to the core. Rarely did a weekend pass when she wasn't out, if not with Donny, then with Jenna or Kim or Whitney or all three and more. But as drawn as she was to her friends, she was allergic to anything academic. At the slightest excuse, she would stay home for the day. "You'll go to school when it's time," Laura insisted, "just like always."

"I can't go to school. I want to be here."

"There's nothing for you to do here. When your father comes home, he'll want to sleep."

"Assuming he hasn't already slept."

Laura felt a flare of indignance. "Where would he have slept?"

Debra's eyes went wide in innocence. "I don't know. Where do *you* think?"

"I don't know! If I did, we wouldn't be standing here at this hour discussing it!" Hearing the high pitch of her voice, Laura realized just how short-tempered she was—and how uncharacteristic that was. "Look," she said more calmly, "we're going in circles. I know nothing, you know nothing. All we can do for the time being is wait for your father to call. If I haven't heard from him by eight or nine, I can start making calls myself." Framing Debra's face with her hands, she said, "Let's not fight about this. I hate fighting. You know that."

Debra looked to be on the verge of saying something before she caught herself and reconsidered. With a merciful nod, she turned and left the room. Laura listened to her footfall on the stair runner, the occasional creak of a tread, movement along the upstairs hall, then the closing of the bathroom door. Only when she heard the sound of the shower did she turn back toward the den.

"Damn it, Jeff," she whispered, "where *are* you?"

•

**Don't Miss These Enthralling Novels
by Barbara Delinsky,
Available from HarperCollins**

Variation on a Theme
When flutist Rachel Busek and rough-hewn private investigator Jim Guthrie meet, they
quickly discover that they are the perfect com-
plement to each other. But there are troubling
pieces of her past that Rachel must uncover before she can trust herself to love Jim completely.

Gemstone
It has been eight years since Sara McCray fled
her husband, Jeff, and an opulent but stifling
life in San Francisco led by her domineering
mother-in-law. Now Jeff has become his own
man, but Sara must decide if she can risk heart-
break again to take a second chance.

The Carpenter's Lady
Writer Debra Barry and carpenter Graham
Reid are two people seeking to forget their
pasts. Debra moves to the country after her
painful divorce and hires Graham to redesign
her new home. But as the house comes to-

gether Debra and Graham start thinking of building a future.

A Time to Love

Arielle Pasteur flies to St. Maarten, to a villa on a private beach, looking for solitude. Instead, she finds herself sharing the hideaway with a man who gives the impression of being an overbearing, scornful egotist. Yet behind the facade lurks a gentleness that makes Arielle question whether it's solitude she really craves.

Rekindled

Here are two Barbara Delinsky novels in one volume. *The Flip Side of Yesterday* and *Lilac Awakening* are two of her favorite romantic stories. Revised by the author and republished by HarperCollins, these stories have been rekindled.

Sweet Ember

Stephanie Wright was a nineteen-year-old camp counselor when she met and fell in love with Douglas Weston, a devastatingly handsome, older tennis instructor. Eight years later Stephanie returns to the camp where she was loved and betrayed, and the truth of that long-ago summer comes to light.

A Woman's Place

Claire Raphael is stunned when, upon her return from a hectic business trip, her husband serves her with divorce papers. He takes the house and custody of the children, too. But Claire has had to fight for every success in her life, and she's not about to give up now.

Finger Prints

Carly is the name she was given by the witness protection program. Even with a new identity, however, she is afraid her enemies will find her. Ryan Cornell is a young attorney who is fascinated by this secretive woman. But Carly cannot so easily reveal herself to another, however great the temptation.

Sensuous Burgundy

Small town assistant DA Laura Grandine and big-city lawyer Maxwell Kraig face off in an explosive courtroom battle. Yet it is the first time either has met their match for wit or will, and neither can deny the power of their attraction.

Together Alone

Emilie, Kay and Celeste have been best friends forever. When their daughters go off to college, however, each mother must find herself as a woman again. Barbara Delinsky expertly interweaves their stories in a beautiful work that is at once moving, romantic and real.

Moment to Moment

From the first moment Russ Ettinger meets Dana Madison, he feels the overwhelming urge to protect her. But Dana has been protected all her life and is determined to be loved only as a strong, independent woman.